Norma Klein

"If You Want, I Can Just Be Your Girl Friend. . . ."

As I was walking home I felt so great about not being married to Eve anymore, I started to run. People must have thought I was crazy. I ran about five blocks, and every time I came to a curb, I gave a big jump, as far as I could go. Finally I got out of breath and slowed down. Then, just as I was getting on the bus, a horrible thought struck me. Having a girl friend is worse in some ways than having a wife. A wife is just someone you happened to marry, but a girl friend is someone you're supposed to really *like*.

I think maybe I'm in worse trouble than I was before.

Books by Norma Klein

A Honey of a Chimp
Hiding
Naomi in the Middle
Robbie and the Leap Year Blues
Tomboy
What It's All About

Available from ARCHWAY paperbacks

Robbie and the Leap Year Blues

Norma Klein

AN ARCHWAY PAPERBACK
Published by POCKET BOOKS • NEW YORK

An Archway Paperback published by
POCKET BOOKS, a Simon & Schuster division of
GULF & WESTERN CORPORATION
1230 Avenue of the Americas, New York, N.Y. 10020

Published by arrangement with The Dial Press
Library of Congress Catalog Card Number: 81-65852

ISBN: 0-671-45216-9

First Archway Paperback printing January, 1983

10 9 8 7 6 5 4 3 2 1

AN ARCHWAY PAPERBACK and colophon are
trademarks of Simon & Schuster.

Printed in the U.S.A.

IL 4+

To the
G O T T E S M A N S :
Brian, Evan, Kay, and Max

Robbie and
the Leap Year Blues

1

"Where are you going, kid? It's Friday. Other side—remember?"

I really feel dumb when Frank, our doorman, has to remind me which side of the building to go to. Usually I remember. I'd say nine times out of ten I do, but sometimes, if I'm thinking about something else, I'll forget. I'm not stupid or anything like that. I'm not even that absent-minded. It's just that for the first eight years of my life we lived on the left side of our building in apartment 7A. That's where my mother still lives now. Then about three years ago my parents got divorced, and my father decided to get an apartment right in the same building. He says he likes the building and the neighborhood and it's convenient to where he works. So *he* got an apartment on the right side. It's divided up so one week I stay with Mom and one week I stay with

1

Dad. That might *sound* confusing, but it's not really. The only confusing thing is when the two of them meet in the lobby. That doesn't happen too often, but when it does, it's kind of awkward and they look at each other like they don't know what to say.

Mom says not to mind. She says divorce is something that happens between parents and I shouldn't feel responsible or anything like that. I don't. I guess they just couldn't get along. That wasn't *my* fault! I get along with both of them pretty well most of the time. But it's funny— since I see them both so much right in the same building, sometimes it doesn't even seem like they *are* divorced.

"Robbie?" Mom was in the bedroom. Usually she isn't home when I get back from school because she's a teacher. She teaches art history at a college in Queens.

"Yeah, hi." I went in. She had a suitcase on the bed and she was packing.

She looked at her watch. "Uh-oh, I better hurry," she said. "The plane leaves at four."

Mom had told me she was visiting this friend of hers over the weekend and that Dad had said it was okay if I stayed with him. Normally my week with him starts Monday. I started to go inside to my room. I decided to do my math homework and, once Mom had left, to watch a little bit of TV. One major problem when I stay at Dad's

2

house is he doesn't have a TV. Well, I mean he has this old one that hardly ever works. He never bothered getting it fixed. Watching something on it that you really want to see is worse than not watching at all. You can hardly see what's on the screen!

"Robbie, I taped Sallie's phone number on the refrigerator," Mom said, looking into my room, "just in case."

"Where does she live?"

"Washington—well, right outside. . . . Is everything okay?"

"Sure."

"When are you going over to Roger's?" Roger is my dad.

"I guess around dinnertime."

Mom swooped over and gave me a kiss. She knows I'm not that big on kisses, at least not the smoochy kind she used to give me when I was little. "Have a good week, hon. See you a week from Monday."

I waited around fifteen minutes after she left before I turned on the TV. By then I was sure she wouldn't come back while I was right in the middle of watching it. Mom's rule is that I can't watch TV till I've finished my homework. I've tried to point out to her that's not a sensible rule. I mean, what if something really good happens to be on at four and you have a lot of homework that night? You could just as easily watch first and do

3

your homework later. Anyhow, when she's not here, I just do it my way and figure what she doesn't know won't hurt her. There are times when it pays to argue with your parents and times when it's easier just figuring out on your own how to do it the way that makes sense.

At around five thirty I took my knapsack and headed over to Dad's side of the building. Now that I'm eleven and go there all the time, the other side doesn't seem like such a big deal. But when I was a little kid, like five or six, it seemed like a whole other world. On Halloween this baby-sitter I used to have, Marjorie Goldsmith, used to take me and my best friend, Chuck, to the other side for trick or treat. Chuck moved away about two years ago and Marjorie Goldsmith went off to college. I saw her over Christmas and she looked like a completely different person. She was wearing makeup and everything. It was sort of a shock.

My father's an editor of science fiction books. It's basically a regular job. He goes to an office and all that and usually he comes home at around six. Sometimes he goes to meetings or parties and isn't there till seven. But his girl friend, Jill, is usually there no matter when I come over because she's between jobs.

It's funny. My parents have the same apartment, the same size, but you'd never know it.

4

They look completely different. My mother is a very neat person. When she goes into a room, you can kind of see her eyeing things that are where they shouldn't be. Like if I leave my sneakers in the middle of the dining room or if she discovers a pile of old comics that I'm saving under the bed or way in the back of the closet, she'll really have a fit. My father, on the other hand, is kind of a slob. His bedroom, the one he and Jill sleep in, has books in piles practically everywhere you turn. Sometimes he doesn't even make the bed! I don't mind that. In fact, I sort of like it. I could stay with him six months and I bet he wouldn't even notice if I never took a bath or had my hair cut or anything. Mom says Dad is used to having women around to pick up after him because he had four older sisters. The only thing is, Jill *doesn't* seem to pick up after him that much. I think she might be even a bigger slob than my father.

"Robbie?"

"Yeah?" I walked down the hall to the bedroom. Jill was lying in bed with the covers pulled up over her. There was a wooden wastebasket with Kleenex in it on one side.

"What are you doing here?" she said. "You really scared me, you know that?"

"I did?"

She sat up and sniffed. She didn't look all that

good. Jill is tall and kind of skinny. Marjorie Goldsmith had more of a figure when she used to be my baby-sitter than Jill does. I guess my father doesn't mind. Otherwise she's sort of pretty. She has light blond hair and blue eyes and sometimes she wears big rimless glasses. Mom calls her Mousie. "Is it Monday?" she asked.

"No," I said. "It's Friday."

"Well, then, I think we're in big trouble."

I just stood there, not getting it.

"Roger's not here. . . . He's away for the weekend."

"Oh."

"See, he had to give this lecture." Jill looked at me uncertainly, like I would know what she was talking about. "In Pittsburgh, of all places. And *I'm* sick as a dog. You better go back and explain to your mother."

"I can't."

"Why not?"

"She's not there."

"Where is she?"

"In Washington, visiting some friend."

"Washington?" She looked like I'd said Alaska.

"Yeah."

"Oh, boy." She frowned. "Didn't they talk to each other about this?"

I shrugged.

6

"What're we going to do? You *can't* stay here, Robbie. You'll get sick. And then your mother'll really kill me."

"I can stay at our place," I said. "It's okay with me."

Actually, I've thought of doing that a lot, just staying by myself, doing whatever I feel like. It'd be fun, just getting up when I wanted, watching TV all day if I felt like it, eating TV dinners and junk food and Cokes.

"All by yourself?"

"Sure, I don't mind. I'd *like* it."

"All weekend?"

It's true two days by myself might almost be too much. One would be perfect.

"They'd kill me; Roger would have my head. . . . Don't you have some friend or someone who could stay with you?"

Jill doesn't have kids. I guess she doesn't realize that most parents would get really nervous leaving two kids alone in an apartment all weekend. They'd probably figure the kids would do dumb, crazy things like set stuff on fire. Or if they're teen-agers, they might figure they'd smoke pot or have wild parties. Not that kids really would do those things, but most parents I ever heard of tend to get pretty nervous, anyway.

I thought a minute. "There's Thor . . . but he's away at his country house."

7

"Oh, no!" She sneezed. "They're going to kill *me,* and here it isn't even my fault. Why don't they talk to each other? Why don't they tell each other what their plans are?"

"Listen, I don't mind staying by myself," I said. "Seriously."

"How about your mother, though? She'd scream bloody murder. . . . Isn't there *anyone?* Like an aunt or something?"

I guess I could have mentioned my Uncle George, Mom's brother, but he and his wife have two-year-old twins. I'd rather sleep out on the street than stay there. "There's Paul," I said finally.

"Who's he?"

"Mom's boyfriend."

Jill brightened up. "Terrific! I didn't even know about him. Is he new or something?"

She made him sound like something Mom bought at a store. "She met him a few months ago," I said.

"Do you know his number?"

"I can look it up." Paul runs an art gallery in SoHo. I know the name of it because Mom and I went down there a couple of times: Perrin's.

I found it in the phone book and called him.

"Where are you, Robbie?" Paul asked after I'd explained what happened.

"At Dad's."

"Okay, well, as a matter of fact, I have to go up

around there to get the girls. I'll see you in half an hour. How's that?"

I didn't even think of asking, "What girls?" I just gave him the apartment number.

"My savior," Jill said, sinking back on the pillows. "I love him. He's saved my life."

Mom says looks don't matter and Dad says they do. You'd think they might think the other way around because Mom is pretty good-looking, as mothers go, and Dad is kind of plump and has frizzy grayish hair. Mom says it's what's inside that counts, that after you've known someone five minutes you forget about how they look.

It'd be hard to forget about how Paul Perrin looks, though. He's around six feet four inches tall and has long blond hair, so light, it's almost white. He dresses in kind of a weird way. Like he'll wear a purple shirt with a bright yellow tie, or a T-shirt with six parrots on it, some of them upside down. He always wears sandals, even in the winter. I think he's about seven years younger than Mom, because once one of her friends was over at our house and saw his picture and said, "Hey, he's darling. Is he out of school yet?'' and Mom said, "Don't be silly. He's thirty-four." Mom is forty-one; she had her birthday around three weeks before. We went out to eat and saw this musical, *Annie,* afterward.

"Listen, I'm *horribly* contagious," Jill said at the door.

"What can you give me that I haven't already had?" Paul said.

"No kidding . . . the doctor said this is some new strain. It's not just *having* it. He said for, like, a month after, you feel you've been run over by a Mack truck."

He grinned. "I think I had that one. . . ."

Jill stood looking at him. She was wearing red-and-white-striped pajamas that came in one piece. It even had a thing in back that unbuttons to go to the bathroom. It even had feet! "I haven't been out of bed all day," she said. "I'm sorry for the way I look. You may be catching something just *standing* there."

Paul came into the living room. "Let me get this straight," he said. "Ellen's in Pittsburgh and what's-his-name's in Washington?"

"The other way around," I said.

"Roger," Jill said. "Not what's-his-name."

"Roger's in Pittsburgh?"

"He's giving a talk," Jill explained, "to—?" She clapped her hand over her mouth. "Isn't that awful? I can't remember to who. And he just told me this *morning.*"

"You're sick," Paul said.

"I'm a mess," she agreed. "Gosh, I hate to do this to you."

"It's nothing. . . . I'll have the girls. They can help out."

"What girls?" Jill asked. I was glad she did, because I'd been wondering.

"The terrible two—Nina and Tracie. I'm divorced and they're . . . They live with my wife."

"Oh, you too?" Jill said. "It seems like everyone . . ." She collapsed in a chair.

"Me too what?"

"Divorce, children, custody . . . everyone I meet. . . . And here *I've* never even been married. Not even once!"

"Well, your generation isn't marrying," Paul said.

"We're not?"

"No, my sister's your age. . . . She says she wants to have some fun before she sells herself down the river."

"Fun?" Jill frowned. "Well, I *guess* I want to have fun. I want to have a family too, though. I want *all* that stuff. I'm a classicist. I like things that last."

"Well." He smiled. "Sure."

"How old are Nina and Tracie?" I asked. I was really beginning to wish they'd let me stay in our apartment alone.

"Let's see—Nina's almost twelve and Tracie's

about to turn ten. Do you want a sexy ten-year-old or an intellectual twelve-year-old? You can have your pick."

"Oh, don't *do* that!" Jill said, like he'd said something awful.

"What did I do?"

"Labeling them that way. People always did that with my sister and me. Then you *get* that way! It's terrible."

"You were the sexy ten-year-old?"

"I wasn't! I just didn't read as much as Nancy. But I wasn't dumb. They used to act like I was really dumb just because I didn't read a book a day like she did."

I guess in a couple of years I'll start getting interested in girls, but right now they aren't exactly a major thing in my life. There are some nice ones and some pretty bad ones, at least judging from the ones in my class at school. I could think of a lot of things I'd rather do than spend a weekend with two of them I didn't even know.

"I wouldn't mind at all staying by myself," I said cheerfully. "I'd be fine."

"What's-her-name would have a fit," Jill muttered.

"Ellen," Paul said. "Her name's Ellen."

"She flies off the handle at anything!" Jill looked at me. "She'd have me drawn and quartered."

13

"No," Paul said.

"What do you mean, no? I know! Listen, once she mailed these tickets to Roger for this concert and they never came and she said I lost them. I never even *saw* them. How could I lose them if I never saw them?"

"Ellen gets nervous sometimes," Paul said, "but she's a good mother. She's good."

They both looked at me. "Yeah," I said.

"It's true," Jill said suddenly. "I've never even been one, so how do I know? I'd be even *more* nervous, I bet. I better not get married. I better not even have kids."

"You get into it," Paul said reassuringly. "Most people don't know how till they do it."

"I wouldn't," she said vehemently. "I'm forgetful. I get sick a lot. Like this is the *third* cold I've had this year. I just pick up germs. If there's a germ anywhere, I pick it up. It's a good thing I'm between jobs."

"What are you between?" Paul asked. He still had his coat on. Jill was sitting cross-legged in a chair with the box of Kleenex in her lap.

"What do you mean?"

"Well, you said . . . What *were* you doing?"

"I wasn't . . . No, it's more. I'm looking . . ." Her voice trailed off.

"For?"

She was looking at him in this nervous way. "I

14

want to be a clown," she said. "I took a course. I'm good. I entertain at children's parties. I put up signs all over the West Side. . . . But I guess I'll have to get a regular job. That won't support me. Do I look like the type?"

"To be a clown? Well, it's hard to—"

I kept trying to imagine Jill dressed up as a clown. You tend to think of clowns as fat old men, the kind you see in circuses.

"I'm good," she said hopefully, looking at both of us. "I can really make people laugh. It's like a gift I have. I'm not being boastful or anything."

"Can you do magic tricks?" I said. Jill had never said anything about being a clown before this. But usually I only see her when my father's around, so we don't talk much.

"Sure." She sighed. "I'd do some now, but I'm feeling so wiped out."

"You know, Tracie's birthday's coming up soon." Paul said. "Maybe she'd like—"

"I can give you references," Jill said, jumping up. "I have a degree and everything."

"Terrific." He turned to me. "So, how about it, kiddo? All set?"

"You know, seriously, I wouldn't mind staying by myself," I said, giving it one more try.

"Don't let the girls scare you," Paul said, putting his arm on my shoulder.

"They don't scare me!" I said. What an idea!

We started out of the apartment.

"Take care . . . what did you say your name was?" Paul asked Jill.

"Gillian. . . . Did you ever see that movie? *Bell, Book and Candle?* She was sort of a . . . not a witch, but . . ." She padded out to the door with us, still clutching the box of Kleenex.

"Would I call you here?"

"Well, I live here, if that's what you mean."

"We'll be in touch, then."

As we waited for the elevator, she poked her head out. "I'm not usually like this. I'm a peppy person usually. I can do backward somersaults. . . ."

Her voice trailed away as the elevator door closed. Paul smiled at me. "Cute," he said. "Have they been living together long?"

"Huh?" I said. I was watching the numbers light up as we went down.

"Have they been living together a long time? Jill and your father?"

"Since Halloween," I said. "She came to his apartment with some little kids and they came in for candy."

"And one thing led to another?" Paul smiled down at me. "Well, that's how it goes, isn't it?"

16

3

There was just one girl waiting outside the building Paul drove up to. She had on one of those duffel coats and she was tall, more like a babysitter almost.

"Hi, Daddy," she said, getting in next to him. I was in the back seat.

"Hi, puss . . . where's Trace?"

"At her gymnastics class!" she said in exasperation. "Where did you expect?"

"Oh, right, I forgot."

"You're late," she said. "You promised her you'd watch. Today's the day you can."

Paul sighed. "Oh, dear. Is there still time?"

"I guess . . . some." She turned around to look at me, but not with a very friendly expression.

"Hi," I said flatly. Why should *I* be friendly if she wasn't going to be?

"That's Robbie," Paul explained.

"What's *he* doing here?"

"Well, you know Ellen?"

"No, who's she?"

"Neens, I know you've heard me mention her," Paul said. "You must've forgotten."

"I don't forget things," Nina informed him.

"Well, be that as it may," Paul said, "Ellen is a good friend of mine and Robbie is her son."

"So, what's he doing *here?*"

"Well, there was a slight mix-up with his parents, so he's going to spend the weekend with us."

"The whole *weekend?*" She looked slightly sick.

I felt like saying I didn't even want to do it, I was being forced to. She reminded me of this girl in our class, Cynthia Ilg, who acts kind of snotty all the time just because she's so smart. I eyed her coolly.

"Nina, come on," Paul said. "In a couple of years you'll be falling all over yourself at the thought of a weekend with a handsome boy like Robbie."

"Sure," Nina said. She turned around to face front. "Big chance."

"I don't like girls that much either," I said.

"It's funny," Paul said. "My best friend was a girl when I was eleven. We used to build dams together."

18

"Dams?" Nina said, like that was the weirdest thing she'd ever heard.

"It was a small country town. That was how we got our kicks in those days." He pulled up in front of a building.

"Was she, like, your girl friend?" Nina persisted. "Did you kiss her and stuff?"

"Nothing like that." He tweaked her hat. "Just good clean outdoor fun."

"Ugh," Nina said, getting out of the car. "Dams!"

I once read a book about building dams. I thought it sounded pretty interesting. These kids built one and then they had a really great place to swim all summer.

Nina's sister, Tracie, was taking a class in the gym of this school. You had to take the elevator down. It was a really gigantic gym, with lots of classes going on in different places.

"There she is!" Nina said. To me she said, "She's the one in red. Don't wave at her or she might mess up."

Tracie was really small for her age. She looked more like eight than almost ten. She had long blond hair almost to her waist and was wearing a red dancing outfit. All these girls were lined up and they had to try and jump over a leather thing, like a saddle. They had to back up, run, and then take a flying leap. Most of them didn't make it. You could tell Tracie wasn't going to make it, but she charged forward like she didn't know that. When she got to the leather thing, she kind of hoisted herself up and fell off the other side onto a mat. Most of them fell. I guess that's why they had the mat.

"It's her first year," Nina explained.

As she came around, Tracie saw us and waved. Then she got back in line. The teacher had them do that jumping thing once more, and then he let them go. He was a really tall Black man. He looked about seven feet tall. That might have been because the girls were so little, though.

Tracie came running over to us. She had bare feet. Her hair was done this funny way. She had a little thin braid hanging right down. It came over one eye, down to her shoulder. "Hi," she said, smiling at me. "I'm Tracie."

"He knows," Nina said. "He's Robbie, and he's going to spend the weekend with us."

"Wow," Tracie said. "Great! . . . Where are you going to sleep?"

"I thought he'd sleep on the foldout couch," Paul said.

Tracie's face fell. "Lucky! . . . Why can't *I* sleep on it?"

"Well, I—"

"You can have *my* bed," she said to me. "I have the top bunk. Please, Daddy. I love the foldout couch *so* much."

"Me too," Nina said. "I love it too. Let him take our room."

"Well, I don't really see what's so wonderful about the foldout couch," Paul said, "but if Robbie doesn't mind—"

"It's okay with me," I said.

Tracie began jumping up and down. "Oh, great! Can we use those special striped sheets too?" To me she said, "We have these sheets with stripes that are every color of the rainbow!"

"They are not," Nina said scornfully. "They're not every single color. Do they have vermilion and burnt sienna?"

"They have a lot of colors," Tracie said.

"Trace, do you want to go change?" Paul said. "I'm double-parked."

"I can just change right here. Here's my stuff." She pulled a sweater over her head, then climbed into a pair of red jeans and struggled into her coat. "Did you think I was good?" she asked me as we went in the elevator.

"What's he supposed to say? He thought you were bad?" Nina said.

"It looked hard," I said.

"It is!" She had really big brownish-yellow eyes. "It's *much* harder than it looks. When you're far away, you think you can make it, but when you're right up in front of it . . . Did you see me do the back flip?"

21

I shook my head.

"Do you want to see? I'm great at that."

"Sure."

She started taking off her coat.

"Right *here?*" Nina said, lifting her eyebrows. "You're going to do it right in the *elevator?*"

"In the lobby," Tracie said, handing her father her coat. "There's lots of room there."

She did six flips one right after the other, landing right on her feet. Boy, she was really light! She hardly seemed to touch the ground. When she was done, she came over to us and put her coat back on. Her face was pink. People with blond hair get that way. Thor's face gets like that when we play tennis together. "What did you think?" she asked.

"Good," I said. "I couldn't do that."

"I used to be able to do two," she said as we went outside. "But now I can do eight."

"I'm on the soccer team," I told her. You don't like to boast about something like that. On the other hand, I wanted to show her there were some things I was good at too.

"Can you roller-skate?" Tracie asked. We got into the car.

"Sort of." I've seen people roller-skating a lot, but I don't have a pair of skates. After Mom and I went to the show the night she had her birthday, we saw this man skating down Central Park West. He was just swooping back and forth with these big red earphones clamped over his ears, dodging around the cars. It looked like he was having a good time.

"If you know how, you can come to my birthday party," she said. "It's going to be a skating party."

"Is that what you want, puss?" Paul asked. "Because today I met a woman who said she does magic tricks and dresses up like a clown. I thought maybe that would be fun."

"Clowns are for babies," Nina said.

"Does she do *good* magic tricks?" Tracie asked.

"I saw a fantastic magician last month," I said. "He made a pigeon disappear right in front of me."

"He probably put him in a box or something," Nina said, facing front.

"He didn't," I said. "He didn't *have* a box."

"Can I have both, Daddy?" Tracie asked. "Roller-skating *and* a magician?"

"Well, we'll see," Paul said. "These things can get kind of expensive, Trace."

"Do you think you want to come?" Tracie asked me.

"I thought you were just having girls," Nina said.

"I am, but he can come. I don't care."

I know I'd feel strange at a party with just ten-year-old girls. "It depends on when it is," I said cautiously.

"I'll send you an invitation," she said. "You can rent skates if you don't have them. It isn't hard to learn."

"Oh, I'm not worried about that," I said.

"You get these knee pads, so even if you fall, it doesn't hurt so much."

"Only babies and teen-agers have boys at their parties," Nina said.

"Since when?" Paul said.

"Most boys are so dumb," she said. "Babies are too dumb to know the difference and teen-age girls just want to dance and kiss people."

"*I* like to dance," Tracie said. "Do you?" She looked back at me again.

"I've never done it," I said.

"I'll teach you," she said. "Daddy has a huge living room. I can do disco."

"You can *not!*" Nina said. All you do is wiggle around and you pretend it's a real step."

"It *is* real." Tracie looked indignant. "I learned it from someone."

Paul had a terrific apartment, the best I've ever seen. It was a loft, one gigantic room divided up into other rooms. But the living room was the size of our gym at school, maybe bigger even. And the furniture was mostly things like big colored pillows and plants like trees. In the middle was a funny metal sculpture of a giraffe, around as big as a real one.

24

"That's Herman," Tracie said. "This friend of Daddy's made him."

She disappeared and came back a couple of minutes later in shorts and a T-shirt, wearing her roller skates. They were the kind like sneakers. She had knee socks on saying Hot Sox. "Maybe you could fit into Nina's," she said. "Then I could teach you right now."

I decided to try, just to show I wasn't scared. I can ice-skate, and you figure roller-skating ought to be easier. But Nina's skates were too small for me. Tracie began skating around the loft. She was really good. Boy, Paul is certainly different from my mother. She'd have a fit if I tried to roller-skate in our living room.

"You're the biggest show-off who ever lived," Nina said as Tracie came skating up to us with one leg out.

"Hey, Daddy, what's for dinner?" Tracie said, sailing right into the kitchen. She didn't pay any attention to Nina.

"It's a surprise," he said.

"Is it meat?"

"Uh-huh."

"Mom thinks we eat too much junk food and not enough good stuff," she told me.

We went back into the living room. Nina was sitting on a pillow on the floor.

"This is the sleep couch," Tracie said. "It's

neat when you fold it out. We'll do it after dinner.
. . . Is your mother Daddy's girl friend?"

I tested out the couch. It was very comfortable. "I don't know," I said.

"Do they go out a lot? Does he sleep over at your house?"

"He doesn't sleep over."

"Well, maybe they're just sort of dating." She sat down next to me on the couch. "Mom only lets the important ones sleep over."

"I hope that one last week wasn't important," Nina said. "He was gross."

"He was okay," Tracie said. "What was wrong with him?"

"He smelled," Nina said. She wrinkled her nose.

"My mother doesn't have people sleep over," I said.

"How long have they been divorced?" Nina asked.

"Three years."

"That's nothing," she said. "Ours have been divored eight years!" She laughed. "Ours have been divorced longer than they were married."

"I don't even remember when they were married," Tracie said. She sounded sad.

"I do," Nina said. "They yelled at each other a lot. . . . Did yours?"

I thought. "Not that much," I said. "But maybe they did it when I was asleep."

"Anyway," Nina said. "I bet the reason your mother doesn't have people sleep over is she isn't really into dating and stuff. Mom said it took her four years till she got interested in men again. She said she was really down on men for a long time."

"Maybe she'll marry Daddy," Tracie said suddenly. She'd just been sitting there, staring off into space, but I guess she was listening.

"He's not the marrying type," Nina said. "That's what Mom says."

"I'd marry him," Tracie said. "I think he's nice."

"You can't marry your own *father,* dodo," Nina said.

"I didn't say I *would,*" Tracie said. "I just said I can imagine someone wanting to."

"Wanting to what?" Paul said, coming over to us. "And, by the way, *diner est prêt.*"

"I'd marry you, Daddy," Tracie said, hugging him. "I think you're really cute. I like your long hairy legs." She looked at him admiringly.

"That's a great reason to marry someone," Nina said. "Because they're cute. Anyway, I thought you wanted to marry that guy in *Superman.*"

Tracie skated ahead of us. "He was nice too," she remembered. "Yeah, he was perfect. He was really strong and friendly *and* he could fly."

"Well, if you want all those things in a man," Paul said, "you may have to wait quite a while.

27

. . . Hon, would you mind taking your skates off for dinner?"

"Sure," Tracie said. She sat down next to me. "You look like the man in *Superman*," she said, "a little,"

"I can't fly," I said.

"That's okay," she said, letting her skates fall with a *klonk* to the floor. "You can do lots of other things, I bet." Her eyes widened. "Wow, is this steak?"

"Genuine sirloin," Paul said, cutting into it.

Tracie watched him. "I wonder how you get sirloin steak," she said. "Do you have to go out and shoot a sirloin cow?"

4

The weekend wasn't as bad as I expected. I slept okay on the bunk bed. It was pretty much like the one I have at home. It was a little babyish because the sheets had these Snoopy characters on them.

Saturday afternoon we went to a theater where Tracie was auditioning for this musical. It was *Annie,* the one I'd seen with Mom. She said her mother saw an ad in the paper that said they were looking for a little girl who could sing and dance. I guess a lot of people saw the ad, because there were mobs of girls at the theater. Tracie's mother met us there. She said we should pick her up at five, when it was over. "Can you remember that? Five?" she said to Paul.

"I think I can remember that," Paul said.

"I have to be home at six," she said. "Six sharp."

"Have no fear," Paul said. "We'll be there on the nose."

"Nina, *you* remember," her mother said. "You have a good memory."

"Sure," Nina said. "I'll remember." To me, as we walked away, she said, "She thinks he's disorganized," pointing to Paul.

"Who me?" Paul said. "The soul of organization, order. . . . Now, where are we going?"

"The movie!" Nina said in affectionate exasperation.

"If Tracie gets into that show, will she quit school?" I asked Paul. There was a guy in my school who was in a movie and they let him study at home.

"Well, first, the chances of her getting picked are pretty slim," Paul said. "They need two kids, and there must have been a couple of hundred trying out."

"She can't even sing!" Nina said.

"She has a certain amount of natural charm," Paul said. "That counts for a lot in show business."

Nina looked at him a long time. "Do I?" she said finally.

"What?"

"Do I have natural charm?"

"Well, sure." He smiled at her. "In a more low-key way."

Nina turned to me. "I wouldn't even want to

be in a show," she said. "I'm going to be an archaeologist when I grow up. I'm going to dig things up in foreign countries. . . . Or maybe I'll be an astronaut. . . . What're *you* going to be?"

Thor wants to be an astronaut too. I used to think of that when I was little, but then you figure you'd have to spend months in this little cabin with not that much to do. And you might not ever come down, if by mistake you pushed the wrong button or something. "I'm gong to be a scientist," I said.

"The kind that invents things to cure people?"

"Yeah."

"What're you going to cure?"

"I don't know." Maybe by the time I'm grown up, they'll have cured everything! Then I guess I'll have to be something else.

"I don't know *what* I want to be when *I* grow up," Paul said. "I'm still working on it."

"You *are* grown-up," Nina said impatiently. "You're something already. You decided."

"You mean, that's it, for life? What a dismal prospect."

"You have to earn money so we can go to school and stuff like that," she said.

"That's just for now," Paul said. "In another couple of years, you and Trace can start earning money to send *me* to school."

"Daddy, don't be silly." Nina looked at me, as though to see if I appreciated how silly he was

31

acting. My father acts like that sometimes too.

"Mom went back to school a few years ago," I said.

"Right!" Paul said. "A perfect example."

Actually, I didn't like it that much when it happened, because Mom was hardly ever around. It was about when Dad moved out, and she said she wanted to be so busy, she wouldn't have time to think. It seemed like all the time she was studying or going to the library or going to classes.

We went to this movie called *Invasion of the Body Snatchers*. It was pretty scary, but good. They kept trying to change these people into pods. They started out as regular people, but then they got covered with this slimy stuff, like rubber cement, and then they didn't act the way they had before, which was scary for the people they knew. Nina kept saying, "Ooh, yuck," every time they changed into pods, and putting her hands in front of her eyes.

"That was really a sick movie," she said enthusiastically when we got out.

"I thought it was great," I said. Mom would never have let me see it. She's pretty strict about what movies I can go to. She thinks a lot of things are too scary or too stimulating. I guess I won't tell her I saw it.

"My father knows a lot about science fiction,"

I told her while we waited for Paul to get the car. "He's an expert."

"Daddy's an expert on art," she said. "Well, I guess they have to be good at something."

"My mother's an expert on art too," I said.

"I guess that's why they like each other," Nina said.

"Yeah," I said. I hadn't thought of that. "What's your mother an expert at?"

"Daddy says she's an expert at kvetching," Nina said. "He says she ought to write a book called *The Art of Kvetching*."

"My parents say things like that about each other too," I said.

"They're not supposed to, you know," Nina said.

"They're not?"

"They're supposed to pretend to like each other . . . for our sakes. But they don't. Sometimes I think they hate each other."

I thought about that. "I don't think mine hate each other," I said. "They just couldn't get along." But then I began remembering this one time they had a fight on Sunday morning. Mom was in the kitchen making French toast and Dad started to say, "Why don't you listen?" and Mom said, "Because I don't want to listen to lies and garbage, you bastard!" Dad saw me standing there and smiled in this sort of nervous way and said, "I am a man of many grievous faults, but a bastard?" "Will you get out of this kitchen?" Mom said. "I *mean* it. I can't take any more of this." Then Dad sighed and rumpled up my hair. He said he was going to take a walk.

We picked up Tracie at the theater. She was standing in front with her mother.

"Where *were* you?" her mother said to Paul.

"We saw *Invasion of the Body Snatchers,*" Nina said. "Boy, it was really gross."

"Were the porno movies all filled up?" Their mother snorted. "We've been waiting here half an *hour.*"

"Sorry," Paul said. "A thousand humble apologies."

"I want them back tomorrow at seven *sharp,*" their mother said. "Can you remember that?"

"I'm going to drop Robbie off then," Paul said. "I'll remember."

"Who's Robbie?"

"That's me," I said.

"He's the son of a good friend of mine," Paul said.

"I thought she moved to Boston."

"That was someone else."

"Oh." She looked at him. "Blessed is he with an infinite supply of good friends. . . . He's staying over with you all weekend?"

"It was sort of an emergency," I said.

"Where's he sleeping?"

"In my bed, Mommy," Tracie said. "Daddy let Nina and me have the foldout couch."

Nina and Tracie's mother looked back at Paul. "Seven *sharp*," she said and turned away.

Paul put his hand up in a salute. She was already walking down the street. I don't think she saw him. "Thy wish is my command." He put his arm around Tracie. "So, how'd it go, sweets? Did you knock 'em dead?"

"I don't know," Tracie said. "They just made me sing 'Tomorrow' and told me to look sad."

"Did you meet the dog?" Nina asked.

Tracie shook her head. "No, he wasn't there."

"He's great. . . . They have this *great* dog in the show," Nina told me.

"Yeah, I know," I said. "I saw it for my mother's birthday."

"How old was she?" Tracie asked. "Ours is thirty-three."

"Forty-one," I said.

"Boy, she's *old!*" Nina said. "Does she have gray hair?"

"Uh-uh."

"Forty-one is so *old!*" she said again. "How come she's so old?"

"Neens, how come you're so nosy?" Paul said. "That's what I want to know. Forty-one isn't old. . . . Ellen is a very lively, energetic person. She—"

"She could be a grandma!" Nina said. "Boy!"

35

I know my parents are a little older than most kids', but they don't act any different so I don't think about it usually. My father's forty-four, but I better not tell Nina that or she'll make some other wisecracks.

Paul took us out for pizza and then we went back to his loft.

"Daddy, you said you'd play the Chess Challenger on the seventh level," Tracie said. She told me, "It's this great game you can play on seven levels. The top level is for people who could play in tournaments!"

"He's not that good," Nina said. "Are you?"

"I used to be," Paul said. "Well, we'll see."

It was sort of interesting. You punched your move on this board and then you waited for the set to tell you what its move was. A lot of times it didn't move right away.

"That's because they have to think up something really good," Tracie said. She was in a long pink nightgown and had big furry slippers on. She was sitting right next to Paul. Nina was reading, but she'd come over occasionally to watch.

"What do you mean, 'they'?" Nina said.

"Whatever's making it work," Tracie said. To me she said, "I think it's a lot of little people. If you play at the first level, just one of them decides what to move, but by the time you get to the seventh level, all seven of them have to decide together. That's why it takes so long."

"What if they don't agree?" Nina said. "What then?"

"I guess they take a vote. . . . Did you ever play it?" she asked me.

I've played chess a couple of times with Thor, but he always beats me. I'm not really that good at it. Maybe I could get better if I practiced. "I never played with one of these," I said. "I never saw one before."

"Maybe when Daddy's done, you can play," she said. "What level do you want to play at?"

"I guess the first one," I said.

"On that one they mostly just take your pawns," she said. "They don't know much about strategy."

It took about an hour, but Paul finally won. The set lit up and said: *I lose*.

"Wow," Tracie said. She hugged her father. "You're a champion! You could win prizes."

"Not exactly," Paul said.

Nina came over. "I don't see what the point of it is if you can win at the seventh level. They ought to make that so hard, no one could win."

"But the set is designed by people," Paul said, "so it has built-in human limitations."

"Do you want to play now, Robbie?" Tracie said to me. "I'll help you, if you want."

It was kind of weird playing against the Chess Challenger. You really started to imagine there *was* someone in there, making the moves. Like, when it took a long time to move, you had the feeling it was thinking: *I'll get him*. The awful thing was I lost! To the first level! Boy, I really felt stupid. "I've only played about six times," I said. That's a lie, really. I've played around twenty times.

"You have to get used to it," Tracie said. "I lost the first time too. . . . I bet next time you'll win."

I thought I'd better go home and practice. The trouble is, a machine doesn't make dumb mistakes. It can't because it isn't human. Sometimes if I play with Thor, he'll just do something dumb.

I didn't have my toothbrush, but Tracie said I could use her electric one because it had four different brushes. "I hope you can sleep over here again," she said. "Do you think you can?"

"I guess, maybe," I said.

"Is your mother going to be mad?" she said. "About what happened?"

"She might be," I said. "I think she'll be mad that Dad forgot to tell her he was going away."

When Mom saw me and Paul Sunday evening, she frowned. "Robbie! Paul!" she said. "What're you doing here?"

Paul explained what had happened.

"You're kidding!" Mom said. "You've *got* to be kidding."

"We didn't mind. . . . He was a big hit with the girls."

38

"I told Roger *ten* times if I told him once," Mom said. "Ten times. It's simply mind-boggling."

"Jill didn't want me to catch her germs," I said. "She had some kind of flu."

"That idiot," Mom said. "I bet she's the one who forgot. Did you meet her?" she said to Paul. "God, I mean, talk about birdbrains!"

Paul smiled. "Well . . ."

"It is *so* classic," she said. "She's, like, a year out of college! If you left her in a room for an hour, she might be able to figure out how to fry an egg."

"She's a clown, Mom," I said. "Did you know that?"

"Yeah, I bet she is," Mom said. "I don't know. I guess everyone has to do something totally foolish once in their lives." She and Paul talked a little bit more. I went into my room.

When he'd left, Mom came in. "Did it really go all right?" she asked, frowning. "Paul's told me all about his girls, but I've never met them. I've seen photos, though. I gather the older one is incredibly bright. . . . The little one looks like a darling. That hair! She's going to be a real heartbreaker when she gets older."

"They were okay," I said.

"Thank heaven there are a few men you can count on!" Mom said.

5

There is one not-so-good thing about this year. You might not know about it since it might not affect your life, but it sure is going to affect mine. I'm going to have to get married! Tomorrow! It's all Thor's fault. See, what happened is this. This year in February there's a day called Leap Year Day. Supposedly on that day girls can ask boys to do anything they want. So some of the girls in my class started asking some of the boys to marry them. Lots of the girls like Thor. He's not that handsome or anything, but he tells funny jokes. Anyway, they like him. So he said he'd marry Emily. She was the one who asked him first. She said she was going to bring in a ring and everything. Then Alix and Penny said *they* wanted to marry him too. He said okay, he'd marry all three of them! Of course, that's not allowed actually, in real life. Anyway, who'd want to marry *three* girls? One is bad enough. Especially Alix. I don't know why anyone would want to marry her. Emily isn't so bad. She takes recorder lessons at the same place Thor does. She's okay, nothing special, but okay. Penny is extremely pretty; she's okay too. I was in this play last year and she played Captain Wesley, who got shot defending his fort against some Indians. I was one of the Indians. She was good. When she got shot, she really doubled over like someone on TV and just lay there for about twenty minutes while the other actors said their parts. Then we had to drag her off by her feet. One time when we were dragging her off, she opened one eye and winked at me. But I don't think anyone in the audience saw.

Anyway, the way this affected me was it gave Eve Lieper the idea of asking me to marry her. She was standing there next to Penny when Penny asked Thor, and she said, "You can marry *me* if you want, Robbie," like she was doing me a favor.

"I don't know," I said.

"I can get a cake from my aunt," she said, like I'd said yes. "She works in this bakery."

"Hey, neat," Penny said. "Can it be a real wedding cake?"

"I don't know. I'll ask her."

"Make it chocolate," Thor said. "That's my favorite kind."

41

"You can't have a chocolate wedding cake," Alix said. She has sort of a whiny voice.

"Why not?" Thor said. "You can have it any way you want."

"Well, I'll ask her," Eve said. "Is chocolate your favorite flavor?" she asked me.

"Yeah, I like it," I said.

"I'm going to wear a dress," Alix said.

"A long white dress?" Penny said. "Or just a regular one?"

"A fancy one."

"Don't make it *too* fancy, or the teachers will catch on."

"What do you want *me* to wear?" Eve asked me. I hadn't even said I wanted to marry her!

"I don't care," I said.

"What's your favorite color?"

"Green."

She frowned. "I don't know if I have something green. . . . Is blue okay?"

"Sure."

I think Thor must really be crazy. He came over to my house after school. It was my week with my father. "How come you want to marry three girls?" I said.

"I don't know," he said. "I didn't want to hurt anyone's feelings."

"Yeah," I said. That's why I didn't say anything to Eve. If she'd asked me when there weren't so many kids around, I would have said

42

no. "So, what're you going to do with all of them?"

"What do you mean?"

"You know . . . how'll it be different from before?"

"It won't be any different," Thor said. "Why should it be different?"

"You mean you won't have to kiss them or go to their houses or anything?"

"If I feel like it, I will," Thor said. "I go to Penny's house sometimes anyway. She lives on my block."

"But do you, like, kiss her or anything?"

"I kissed her once," he said. "It wasn't anything that great. . . . Once we took our clothes off."

"You did?"

"Yeah . . . she said she wanted to see how a boy looked without clothes on. She doesn't have any brothers or anything."

I think I'd be embarrassed to do that. "Did she take *her* clothes off too?" I just couldn't imagine Penny doing that.

"Yeah."

Boy, he was so calm! What'd she look like?" I said.

"Okay," Thor said. "She doesn't have a figure yet."

"Yeah," I said. You can tell that.

"Eve does."

"I don't like her that much, though."

"So, you don't have to like her. . . . Just say you're curious what a girl looks like without her clothes."

Once I saw Jill without clothes. It was my mistake. She was doing these yoga exercises in the bedroom and she likes to do them without any clothes on. I didn't know that. She had her eyes closed. I closed the door right away.

After Thor left, I just sat there gloomily till Dad came home. Boy, I wish they had never invented Leap Year Day! At least it's only every four years.

"What're you looking so glum about, Robbie?" Dad asked at dinner.

"I don't know," I said, not looking at him.

"Problems at school?"

"Sort of."

"With math?"

I shook my head. I guess I wouldn't have minded telling him so much if Jill hadn't been there.

"Maybe he has a girl friend," Jill said. She was wearing her glasses. It made her eyes look big and round.

I just kept chewing my food.

"Is that it?" Dad said. "Is it something about a girl, Robbie?"

"Sort of."

"*I* had a boyfriend when I was eleven," Jill

said. "He was thirteen and he had this paper route? I used to stand waiting for him to deliver that paper all afternoon, rain or shine. I really liked him. You know what was funny? He had one blue eye and one brown eye. But he was really cute anyway."

"It's on account of Leap Year Day," I explained.

"What is?" Dad got up to clear the dishes away.

"Well, see, on Leap Year Day girls can ask boys to do anything they want."

"Umm-hmm?"

"So this girl in my class, Eve, asked me to marry her." I looked at both of them. "Thor's marrying *three* people! He's really crazy."

"Do you like her?" Jill asked. "Is she pretty?"

"She's okay."

Dad smiled. "You know, you don't have to marry her just because she asked you, Rob."

"I know." I tried to explain. "But she said it when all these kids were standing around. I didn't want to be mean. . . . Anyway, I never even said I would. She acted like I said yes, when all I said was, 'I don't know.' "

"She must like you a lot," Jill said. She smiled.

"I don't know," I said.

"Gosh, *I* think that's exciting," she said. She looked at Dad. "Don't you, sweetie?" Then suddenly her face fell. "I'll be the only member of

45

this household who's never been married. There must be something wrong with me."

"Oh, your generation isn't marrying," Dad said. "You're learning from looking at our generation."

"That's just what *he* said," Jill said.

"Who?"

"Your—Ellen's boyfriend. The one who took Robbie for the weekend? He said I was like his sister. He said she wanted to have some fun before she sold herself down the river."

"What's he like?" Dad asked.

"Who?"

"Ellen's—"

"Tall," she said. "Really tall."

"I gather he's a bit younger."

"Than who?"

"Well, than Ellen."

"Oh." Jill looked at me. "He didn't *seem* that young," she said. "He has these two daughters."

"He's thirty-four," I said.

"That's not *so* young," Jill said.

"Yes, it is," Dad said.

"*I'm* just twenty-four," she reminded him.

"Well, women mature faster," Dad said. He gave me a bowl of chocolate pudding. "Robbie, just take it in stride . . . but remember, when it's the real thing, don't say yes when you mean no. A lot of guys have found themselves with six kids and a mortgage with that kind of attitude."

46

After dinner I got this great idea. Maybe Thor will trade Penny for Eve. He said he thought Eve had a figure and Penny didn't. That's true in a way, but I like Penny a lot better. And what does he care? He has three of them. I called him up and told him my idea.

"Well, I don't know," he said.

"How come? You said you thought Eve wasn't so bad."

"It's not that. I just think Penny would mind."

I swallowed. "She likes me," I said, remembering how she winked at me that time. "I think."

"Sure," he said. "Only, well . . . listen, you stick to Eve. It'll be okay."

"I just don't like her that much," I said. "I hardly ever *talked* to her!"

"She's shy or something," he said. "Anyway, she must like you or she wouldn't have asked you."

"Yeah," I said.

I hung up, feeling depressed. Boy, Thor is lucky. With three of them, if he doesn't like one, he has another one. In that way maybe having three is better than one. But I think having none is the best of all!

6

We arranged to have the weddings during lunch hour. If the weather is not so cold, we go to this park near the school and they let us roam around doing pretty much what we want. Patrick said he'd be the guy who does it, like the minister.

One thing that was really strange was that Eve had put on real makeup. Lipstick and everything. She looked like a teen-ager almost. "Is this dress okay?" she asked me.

It just looked like a regular dress to me. "Sure," I said.

"There's some green in it," she said, "even though it's mostly blue."

Alix was wearing a really fancy dress with a lace collar like she was going to some kind of party. I really can't stand her. At least Eve is more sort of quiet. That might be because she comes from this foreign country, Venezuela.

48

She's American and all that, but her father worked there. She came in the middle of the year, and she knows Spanish.

Alix said, "Wait a second." She took this lace handkerchief out of her knapsack and put it on her head. It was sunny but pretty windy, so she had to hold it in place. Penny was just in jeans and her duffel coat like usual.

"I can play the wedding march," Emily said. "I brought my recorder."

"But you're getting married!" Alix said. "How can you?"

"Afterward," Emily said. "After we do the getting married part."

I looked over at Thor. He grinned. "Hey, Patrick, you going to do your stuff?"

Patrick stood in front of us. "Well, let's see," he said. He frowned, like he was giving an oral report at school. "Do you, Thor, take these three girls to be your—" He stopped.

"Lawful wedded wives," Penny said.

"I thought we'd do it separately for each person," Alix said, frowning.

"But that'd take too much time," Penny said. "Lunch hour'll be over then."

"But what if one of us wants to get divorced and the other ones don't?"

Penny shrugged. "That doesn't matter."

Patrick cleared his throat. "So, anyhow . . . do you do all that stuff?"

"What stuff?" Emily said. "You didn't say."

"To have and to hold, for richer or poorer, in sickness and in health," Penny said, like she'd memorized it.

"Yeah," Patrick said. "All that."

"Boy, you're not even doing it!" Alix said. "You're not doing it *right!*"

"You're supposed to say to honor and obey," Emily said. "My sister got married and they said that."

"That's old-fashioned," Penny said scornfully. "No one says obey anymore. That sounds like a dog. Do you promise to fetch and carry, roll over, play dead . . . ?"

Thor barked. "Arf, arf."

"Down, boy," Patrick said.

"Do the 'I do' part," Alix said impatiently. "We won't even have time to eat the cake."

"Okay, so do you?" Patrick said, looking at Thor.

"Yeah," Thor said. "I do."

"*I* do," Penny said.

Alix smiled in this kind of sickening way, like she was really getting married. "I do."

Emily just stood there.

"Go on," Alix said. "Say it!"

"I'm not sure," Emily said.

Alix sighed. "Oh, boy! Come on, make up your mind."

Emily looked worried. "I guess I don't want

50

to." She looked at Thor. "Is that okay?" she said. "We can still be friends."

"Sure," Thor said.

"I just—" She looked at us. "I just wasn't sure."

"So, kiss them," Patrick said. "Go to it, man!"

Thor kissed Penny first and then Alix. He kissed them right on the mouth. He kissed Emily too, even though he didn't have to. I guessed I'd have to do that with Eve too. My heart started thumping.

Patrick waved his hand around in the air. "I now pronounce you man and wife."

"Wives," Penny said. She grinned. "Hey, that wasn't so bad."

"We're next," Eve said. She looked a little scared.

I kept thinking about who it was who invented Leap Year Day. I bet he never stopped to think about all the trouble he'd get people into by inventing a day like that. He probably just thought it sounded funny.

Patrick said the same thing for us that he had for Thor and Penny and Alix. I just stood there.

"Kiss her!" Alix hissed.

"Okay," I said. I was going to. I just wanted time to think about it a minute. I leaned over and kissed Eve really quickly. She smelled nice. It wasn't so bad.

51

"You're wearing perfume," Alix said to Eve afterward.

"Yes." She turned red.

"It's nice. . . . I wish *I'd* thought of that. My mom has lots."

"So where's the cake?" Patrick said. "I'm starving, man."

"You didn't even get married," Thor said. "What're *you* so hungry about?"

Eve got the cake out of the box. It was a chocolate cake. On the top was one of those plastic things showing a man and a woman holding hands. "It's all chocolate," she said. She gave me the first piece.

"Hey, no fair!" Patrick said.

"He's her husband, dope," Penny said. "She can give him the first piece if she wants."

The cake was really good. *That* part of getting married I liked. We sat around till Mr. Pool blew the whistle for us to go back inside.

"Hey, wife," Thor said, waving his hand. "Fetch me my knapsack."

Penny stared at him, hands on her hips. "Arf, arf," she said.

"*I'll* get it," Alix said. Can you believe she actually carried Thor's knapsack back to school?

He winked at me. "Got to train 'em young," he said.

At dinner Dad and Jill asked me how it had

gone. I'd kind of been hoping they'd forget. "It was okay," I said. "The cake was good."

"Two married men," Jill said. "I'm living with two married men. That sounds kind of kinky, doesn't it?" She looked solemn. "I bet I'm *never* going to get married."

"Sure you will," Dad said.

"Yeah?"

"There's nothing worse than rushing into things," he said, "doing things before the time is right."

"I guess." She stared off into space with a dreamy, sad expression.

"Is that what happened with you and Mom?" I asked.

He smiled. "Well . . . it's complicated."

"But you were over thirty!" Jill said. *"And* you lived together for three *years!"*

I didn't know that.

"You must have known *everything* about each other by then," Jill said. "And it *still* didn't work."

"What can I say?" Dad said. "No one can predict."

I wonder if Jill wants to marry my father. I never thought of that before. I don't think Mom would like it that much. I don't know how I'd feel about it either. She's okay, she's a nice person and all that, but I don't think she's so much the mother type. I can't imagine telling people I had a mother who was a *clown!* They'd think I was really crazy. I know kids whose parents are divorced where they got married again. So, like, I know it does happen. But it seems to me they ought to at least wait a while. Maybe five or ten years. First, it takes a while to get used to the idea that they're divorced. It would be kind of a shock if they went and got married right away. Also, you figure they weren't that great at being married or they wouldn't have gotten divorced, so they ought to think about that too. They ought to look at it from all angles, like Mr. Pool tells us to do in our social studies reports. My father is basically a rational person. I think he does try and look at things from all angles.

"So, Robbie, I think it's about time for lights off," he said later when I was reading in bed. "You've had a pretty big day."

It seemed like all that had happened a long time ago. "Dad?"

"Umm-hmm?"

"Are you and Jill going to get married?"

He laughed. "No. What gave you that idea?"

"No, it's just . . . sometimes people do after they've been divorced."

"Oh, of course. . . ." He stood there, looking uncertain. "Jill is a lovely person," he said. "I'm extremely fond of her, but . . . she's very young."

"Yeah." I got under the covers. "Anyway, she doesn't seem so much the mother type to me."

"Oh, I don't know," Dad said. "I think, under the right circumstances, Jill would be a fine mother."

For someone else, I thought, not for me.

"I'm pretty happy with things just as they are now," Dad said. "Why change things when they're going well?"

"Sure," I said. "That's what I think."

7

I was really relieved about one thing. Everybody seemed to completely forget about the thing of getting married once it was over. It was exactly like the time we had this big election for governor of our class. Thor nominated me and I went home and made all these posters, telling kids to vote for me, and then I got elected, along with some other kids, and we had, like, one meeting and that was it. That time I was really disappointed, but this time I was glad.

Two weeks later Eve came up to me after school and asked if I wanted to go out for pizza with her.

"I don't have that much money," I said.

"That's okay," she said. "I have some."

There's this pizza place near our school where some of the older kids, the ones in high school, go with girls. I go there with Thor sometimes. I got a plain slice with a Coke and Eve got the same thing only with a Tab.

"My mother thinks I might begin to get fat now that I'm eleven," she said, pointing to the Tab.

"You don't seem that fat now," I said. Actually, she is a little fat, but not too much, more plump.

"She says when she was my age she got fat and it might be hereditary." She bit into her slice of pizza. "She says it can't hurt to be careful."

I couldn't think of anything to say. I bet Thor could. He's the kind of person who's always talking. He never seems to worry if what he says sounds right or not.

"The thing is," Eve said, "you know how we got married two weeks ago?"

"Yeah?" I hoped nobody near us was listening.

"Well, I was thinking . . . I'm just not so sure." She looked at me with a worried expression. "I think maybe I don't want to be married anymore."

"That's okay." Boy, what a relief!

"It's just . . . we *are* kind of young."

"Sure."

"If we were, like, in high school."

"I guess it was more just sort of like a joke," I said.

Eve looked indignant. "But it shouldn't be," she said. "Getting married is a serious thing!"

"Yeah."

"I'm just going to get married once. I'm not going to marry lots of different people. . . . Are you?"

"What?"

"Do you think you'll marry one person or lots of different people?"

"One person, I guess." I'm not sure I'm getting married at all actually, but this didn't seem like a good time to mention that.

Eve smiled at me. She has a nice smile. "I'm glad you don't mind," she said. "It's not that I don't like you or anything."

I was looking at the crust of her pizza. To me the crust is the best part, but some people don't like it. "Are you going to eat your crust?" I said finally.

"You can have it," Eve said. "You look like you don't have to worry about being fat."

My mother is always worried about my being too thin. I guess mothers always worry about something. "It's good," I said. "They have good crusts here."

"If you want," Eve said, "I can just be your girl friend."

I took a swallow of my Coke. "Sure," I said.

She beamed.

As I was walking home I felt so great about not being married to Eve anymore, I started to run. People must have thought I was crazy. I ran about five blocks, and every time I came to a curb, I gave a big jump, as far as I could go. Finally I got out of breath and slowed down. Then, just as I was getting on the bus, a horrible thought struck me. Having a girl friend is worse in some ways than having a wife. A wife is just someone you happened to marry, but a girl friend is someone you're supposed to really *like*.

I think maybe I'm in worse trouble than I was before.

I don't get a lot of mail these days. My grandfather writes me from San Francisco sometimes, but that's about all. A few years ago I used to send away for stuff, free things I read about in magazines. Practically every day I'd get something in the mail. But it got sort of dull. Most of those things—plastic animals and dumb records—were a gyp, even if they were free. They made them sound great in the ads, but they didn't look anything like that when they came.

One day when I got home from school, I saw this letter for me on the bench in the hall. I opened it up. It was an invitation to a birthday party. It was from Tracie Perrin. It said to meet for roller-skating at this place downtown. Inside she'd written a note on a separate piece of paper.

Dear Robbie,

Do you remember me? Do you remember I

said I was going to be 10? Well, I am and I was wondering if you could come to my party. Don't worry about the roller-skating. I can teach you how.

Tracie ♡

P.S. The heart isn't because I want to be sexy. That's just the way I sign my name.

P.S.2. I beat the Chess Challenger once. They beat me twice!

I never thought life would get this complicated when I was eleven. It seems like nothing much happened for most of my life and now all of a sudden everything's happening. I can't go to a party for ten-year-old girls. If it was a girl in my class, it'd be different. But here it'll be girls I don't even know. I figured I better think of a really good excuse, like I was exposed to measles. Yeah, that's a good one. Nobody wants to get measles, especially not on their birthday. I called Tracie up. She answered the phone.

"Uh, Tracie?"

"Oh, hi, Robbie. Did you get my invitation?"

She must be good at remembering people's voices! "Yeah," I said. "I—"

"It's going to be great!" she said. "We're going to have roller-skating *and* a magician! And who-

60

ever can beat the Chess Challenger will get a special prize. Have you been practicing?"

"I was exposed to measles," I blurted out.

"Oh, gee, I'm sorry," Tracie said. "I had them last year. They're not so bad. It's just like a cold and you itch a little."

Oh, wow. I never thought of that, that she might've *already* had them! "I thought maybe I better not come," I said, "because your friends might get measles that way."

"Oh, no," she said cheerfully. "They *all* had them last year. This boy in our class had them and infected everybody! The whole class got them. One day only three people showed up for school. . . . Personally, I think some people were just pretending."

I didn't know what to say.

"So listen, I'll see you Saturday, a week from Saturday."

"Okay," I said.

Boy, I'm really dumb! There's one rule I learned: Always have a backup excuse. That's what Dad says. He says you should think things through and have an invincible line of argument. Now what am I going to do?

"Oh, hi, Robbie," Mom said. She still had her coat on. She must've just come in. "Who's the invitation from?"

It was lying on the bed. I showed it to her, just

61

the invitation, not the letter. "How sweet," Mom said. "I guess she really did like you. Paul said she did."

"Mom, the thing is, it's just going to be girls—*ten*-year-old girls."

"So?"

"Well, it's just I'd feel kind of funny if any of my friends saw me."

Mom laughed. "Honey! Who's going to see you? And so you're popular with girls? Is that such a tragedy?"

Maybe mothers just don't understand that it's different if it's girls not your own age. Ten is really young. It's just fifth grade. "Anyhow, I don't know how to roller-skate," I said.

"You'll learn in three seconds. Look how good you are at ice-skating. Anyone who can ice-skate can roller-skate."

Actually, I think that's true. I just sat there. I couldn't think of any other excuse.

Suddenly Mom said, "Hey, listen, I have a super idea! I'll come with you." While I was looking at her in horror, she said, "I was terrific at roller-skating when I was your age. Oh, it was totally different then. We just had these measly little skates that you had to fasten on with a skate key. But I bet it would come back to me. Don't you think it would?"

"Sure, I guess."

If I thought I was badly off before, now I really

have problems. Imagine if a bunch of kids from my class show up and there I am with my mother, who hasn't skated since she was eleven, *and* a whole pile of ten-year-old girls. Boy, I wish there was some place I could go and *really* be exposed to measles. Even being sick wouldn't be as bad as this. "Are you going to stay for the whole party?" I asked uneasily.

Mom considered. "No, I don't think so. I have some shopping to do. I'll just whirl around a bit and then vanish." She turned to go. "I'll call Paul right now and let him know."

8

Thor said he'd show me how to roller-skate. He has new roller skates that he got for Christmas. I'm going to go to his house Tuesday after school.

Our last class Tuesday is kind of dumb. It's called Child Care. You have to take it, whether you're interested or not. The point of it is to show you what babies are like, in case you ever have one or if you baby-sit and, instead of a regular child, the couple has a baby. In each class they show us how to do one thing, like put diapers on the baby or give it a bath. What's unusual about this class—I'm not saying good, just unusual—is they give us real babies to practice on. Mostly they're babies that belong to families of kids who go to our school. Their mothers or baby-sitters bring them at the beginning of each class and pick them up at the end.

Two people share a baby. Thor and I got one

called Tigran. You've probably never heard that name before. His mother explained to us that he was named after an Armenian king called Tigran the Great. Thor calls him Tiger. I personally don't think Tigran knows his real name. You can call him anything and he grins at you. He's a pretty easygoing baby. I'm glad of that. Some of the babies other kids got stuck with cry all the time, no matter what.

We had some trouble with Tigran this time. Today we learned to give them a bath. That doesn't *sound* too complicated, but evidently not all babies like water. They gave each team a plastic container like a small tub. First we had to undress our baby and put him in. Some kids have girl babies—it's fairly even. They didn't let us pick. They just handed out the babies in the first class. I was glad we got a boy. I'd have felt funny with a baby girl, I think. I put Tigran in the tub. It had some warm water in it already.

"There you go, Tiger," Thor said, taking the soap. "You're going to get nice and clean. How about that?"

He looked pretty clean already, like maybe he'd had a bath before he came. "Who's going to hold him?" I said.

"You can."

"Okay, but that means you have to shampoo his hair."

"Sure."

65

Tigran at least *has* hair to shampoo. Lots of the babies are totally bald. You'd think by nine months they'd have had a chance to grow some hair, but evidently not. Tigran has black hair, a lot of it. It stands up around his head in curls. He has big black eyes that stare right at you. He didn't seem to mind the bath part; where we ran into trouble was rinsing off his hair. It was Thor's fault. He put on too much shampoo. Then he began pouring water over Tigran's head. I was tilting him back so the water wouldn't get into his eyes. The teacher, Ms. McBride, told us most babies hate getting water, especially with soap in it, in their eyes.

"You're getting water in his ears," I said.

"So?" Thor said. "He doesn't mind. Do you, Tig?"

"Thor, will you hurry up? He's heavy!"

"Take it easy. . . . Do you want to switch? I can hold him and you rinse."

"Okay." I gave Tigran to Thor, who tilted him back. "Tilt him back more," I said.

"I can't. . . . Listen, just pour the water, will you? Don't make such a big production out of it."

"Okay, here goes." I scooped up a glass of water and poured it over Tigran's head. Only instead of it running just down his back and neck, it spilled right over his face. He let out a piercing yell.

"Terrific, Rob," Thor said. "Perfect aim." Tigran was splashing the water in the tub with his hands like he was really angry.

"You didn't tilt him enough," I said defensively.

"I did. . . . You just dumped the water right over his head. . . . Hey, Tig, calm down, okay? Rob, do that act he likes. Maybe that'll cheer him up."

Tigran likes it when I make this monster face. I bare my teeth and pretend to snarl at him. Usually he laughs and laughs, but this time he kept right on crying.

"His mother's going to be really mad at us," I said. "He'll never want to have his hair washed again."

Just then Ms. McBride came over. She likes to let us do everything ourselves, but she watches from the front of the room. "How are things going, boys?" she said.

Tigran stopped crying and looked at her.

"We got some water in his eyes," Thor admitted, "but I think he's okay now."

"Of course he is," Ms. McBride said briskly. "A little water never hurt a baby. Remember, boys, babies are tough. Don't be afraid of them."

"We're not," I said. Imagine being afraid of a baby! What does she think we are? "We just didn't tilt him enough."

"You have more of a problem because Tigran has so much hair," Ms. McBride said. "Just try it once more. I think most of the soap is out."

But Tigran didn't want to tilt back at all after that. He just sat straight up in the tub, looking at us suspiciously. At least he'd stopped crying. I kind of smoothed some water down his head with my hand to get the rest of the soap out.

When Tigran's mother came to pick him up, you'd never have known anything bad had happened. "Ma!" he said when he saw her. He doesn't know too many words yet, but Ms. McBride said that's the way babies are at this age.

"We had a little problem washing his hair, Mrs. Lambert," Thor said, "but it worked out okay."

Tigran's mother sighed. She has a French accent, but you can understand her, except when she speaks French. "I cannot wash his hair. He hates the water in his eyes. It is a big, *big* problem." She looked at Tigran. "You were good today, Tigran? You made no trouble?"

"Ma," Tigran said.

"No, he wasn't any trouble," Thor said. "Were you, Tig?"

When we were on our way to his house, Thor said, "I wonder what country Tigran comes from."

"I thought she said the Middle East someplace."

"He's not so bad . . . compared to some of them. But I'm glad we don't have any babies in our family."

"Me too," I said.

"My mother went through this stage of saying she wanted a girl and maybe we ought to adopt one. She even went to some agency about it. . . . But I guess my father talked her out of it."

I nodded. "Mine would've liked a girl if they'd had another one. But she said when the first one is born, you just want them to be okay, you know, like not have eight toes on one foot or stuff like that."

"I guess they figured your personality was weird enough, huh?" Thor looked at me suspiciously. "Hey, how come you have to learn to roller-skate?"

"I don't have to—I just figured I might as well learn."

"It's easy."

"I know. I just thought you could show me, like, how to turn and slow down."

"I'm not such an expert," Thor admitted, "but I'll show you what I know."

The trouble was, Thor's skates didn't fit me. They were too small. I guess if they'd been too big, I could've put them on, but I couldn't get them on my feet.

"Well, look," Thor said. "I'll put them on and you can watch me, okay?"

Thor doesn't have a very big room. He rolled up the rug and shoved it in the corner. "Here goes," he said, and he began skating around the room. "Now, when you want to turn . . . " he began.

Just then the door opened. It was Thor's mother. "Thor, what are you *doing?*" she said.

"Showing Robbie how to roller-skate," Thor said. "He needs to learn how."

"In the house?" She looked angry. "You have more sense than that. Teach him outside, in front of the building."

"But it's raining, Mom."

"You may *not* roller-skate in the apartment and that's final!"

After she'd left, Thor looked at me. "Sorry," he said.

"My mother is the same way," I said. "It's okay."

We sat there a minute in silence.

"Listen, I have an idea," Thor said. "Let's go down to the lobby. I'll do it there."

"Will they let you?"

"Sure. . . . They used to have this big rug down, but they took it up. Anyhow, the door-man's a friend of mine. He won't make a fuss."

Thor and I went down to the lobby of his house. There was a marble floor. The doorman, a little guy with a mustache, was sitting near the front door listening to a transistor radio. "Pablo," Thor said, "this is my friend, Robbie. He has to

70

learn to roller-skate, see? So I'm just going to show him a couple of things. Okay?"

Pablo nodded and smiled. *"Sí,"* he said. "Is okay."

Thor began skating around the lobby. "Wow, this surface is tricky," he said, skidding. Don't watch this, Rob." He started shooting down the lobby really fast. Just as he was about to turn, the elevator door opened. A lady came out and, maybe because she wasn't looking up, banged right into Thor. I thought he'd fall down, but instead he skated backward, with the lady hanging on to him for dear life. They zoomed down the lobby until they reached this bench at the end. Then Thor sat down with a thump and the lady sat down in his lap.

Pablo got up and came running over.

The lady looked at Thor indignantly. She had gotten up and was brushing herself off. "What were you doing?" she said.

"I'm sorry, Mrs. Taub," Thor said. "See, my friend, Robbie, has to learn to skate and it's raining out and my mother doesn't want me to skate in my roon, so I thought—"

"Pablo," Mrs. Taub said, "there could have been an accident. I could have been badly hurt."

"Sí," Pablo said, looking worried. "He goes too fast. He cannot stop."

"Well, then he shouldn't be doing it." She

71

looked at Thor. "You're old enough to know better, young man," she said, and walked out the front door.

Thor sighed. "I guess we better go back upstairs," he said. "I'm sorry, Pablo, I didn't mean to get you into trouble."

Pablo looked at the lobby floor. "Is not good surface for skating. . . . You not see lady?"

"Yeah, that's the thing," Thor said. "I didn't even *see* her!"

"She nice lady," Pablo said. "She not complain."

"Good," Thor said.

Upstairs in his room Thor put his skates away. "Well, you get the general idea," he said.

"Sort of," I said.

"You just kind of do it. Go slow in the beginning. . . . How about a game of chess before you go home?"

"Okay." I sat down on the floor while Thor got the chess set out of his closet.

"I got a terrific book out of the library," Thor said. "It shows a lot of great openings for chess."

"Can I borrow it?"

"Sure."

At least if I can't roller-skate, maybe I can get good enough at chess to beat that chess computer. I know I could never beat it at the top level like Paul Perrin did, but I think I can learn to beat it at the bottom level. That's good enough.

9

The morning of the party I got a brainstorm. About two winters ago, when it was really cold, down to zero, Mom got me this kind of strange hat. It's called a face mask and it covers your whole head and face except for two holes for your eyes and a hole for your mouth so you can breathe. By the time she got it, the weather was more back to normal, so I never wore it. But I figured if I brought it I could keep it in my pocket and if I saw anyone from my class, I could just whip it out and put it on. There's no way *anyone* could recognize me with *that* thing on.

The skating place was way downtown along the Hudson River at a pier. Right next to it there was a big ocean liner that I guess was going to take people to Europe or someplace. It was pretty windy. Really, it was just like a regular place to skate except that they had two big speakers with loud music coming out of them. When you skated past them, the music got really loud, and when you skated down toward the river, it got softer. You couldn't make out the words much, but it was kind of rock music about love and sex and stuff.

I rented a pair of skates from a man in a booth. They had my size. They were the kind like ice skates that come partway up your leg. Tracie had about five friends, and they were all really good skaters, despite being ten. They took off like demons and were racing around, holding hands, in one long line. There was just this one friend of hers who didn't even want to rent skates. She just sat and watched the whole time.

I went around the first few times sort of slowly. Tracie came up to me and stopped by going around in a half circle. She was wearing a shiny jacket with red arrows on it. "Do you want to skate with me?" she said.

"Okay," I said.

She took my hand. "You're doing good," she said.

The trouble is, it's hard skating with another person. They do it a different way from you, but *you* have to try and do it *their* way. All of a sudden Tracie fell. She fell right in front of me, and I fell right on top of her! I know I wouldn't have fallen if she hadn't done that.

"Are you okay?" she said, getting up.

"Sure, are you?" My knee felt a little sore. "Maybe I better try skating by myself," I said, hoping she wouldn't mind, "till I get the hang of it."

"Okay." She didn't seem to mind.

After that all of a sudden I caught on. I think it was when I went around for about the tenth time. All of a sudden I was doing it. I wasn't thinking of whether I'd fall or if I could make the turns. I just did it. It was a great feeling. I stopped looking down at my feet and looked around. It was a funny group of people. Like with ice-skating, there were some people in the middle doing fancy things. One lady in red slacks and a red jacket was doing some kind of dance step, wiggling back and forth. And this little guy with a beard was into some kind of racing step. He'd take two or three long swooping steps and then glide halfway around the rink.

I saw Mom. She was skating with Paul. They looked kind of funny, because she was wearing this bright-red hat with a pom-pom on it and red mittens and a blue coat, and he was wearing a bright purple jacket and a long orange scarf that blew out in back of him. Mom seemed to be doing pretty well, better than I'd expected. I guess she remembered from when she was a kid. She looked really happy.

"Hi, sweetie," she said as they passed me. "Isn't this fun?"

"Yeah, I like it," I said.

I'm not sure I like it as much as ice-skating, but I do like it. The thing is, with ice-skating it seems more like a skill because you're balancing on a thin piece of metal. Here you figure practically anyone could do it, unless they were really unco-ordinated.

You know how sometimes everything is going well—you have nothing to worry about—and then all of a sudden some dumb thing happens to spoil everything? Well, just as I came around the bend, down by the place where they rent skates, I saw this guy Joey from my school. Actually he's in seventh grade, but he knows me because we take the bus together and he's on the soccer team with me. I lowered my head and skated past him real fast. Then I skated as fast as I could to the far end of the rink. I stopped and pulled the face mask out of my pocket. It was kind of a typical March day, windy and a little cold. Not the kind of day you'd normally wear a face mask, even if you had one, but at least it wasn't, like, eighty degrees. I put it on. It was a little scratchy, but I felt better.

But as I skated around again, Nina skated over to me. "What's that thing you have on?" she asked. "You look like Batman or something."

I guess the trouble was she saw me before, so she knew who I was. We were skating past the place Joey was sitting with his friend. "It's a face mask," I said softly through the hole. Probably he couldn't hear, because the music was so loud, but I figured I might as well be careful.

"What's it for?"

"Well, I was exposed to measles and they said it'd . . . keep the germs off other people."

"Huh?" She looked at me suspiciously.

Just then Mom skated by, alone. "Robbie, why're you wearing your face mask?" she said. "It's not that cold."

"It's to keep the germs away," Nina said. "He was exposed to measles."

"You didn't tell me that," Mom said, starting to get all excited. "When *was* that? Didn't they send a note home?"

"I guess I left it in school," I said.

"Goodness—do you feel okay?" I could tell she would've put a hand on my forehead to see if I had fever except I had the face mask on.

"Yeah, I feel fine," I said.

Tracie and two of her friends skated over.

"Hey, neat!" Tracie said. "What a great hat."

"It's to keep germs off," Nina said.

"Can I wear it?" Tracie said. "You can wear mine." She offered me this stocking hat she had.

"You don't *have* germs," Nina said. "He was exposed to measles, dope. Do you want everyone here to get sick?"

"*We* had measles," Tracie said. "Please, just for a second."

"You can try it on when we get to your house,"
I said. Boy, this was getting to be more trouble
than it was worth. Out of the corner of my eye I
could see Joey skating past. Luckily I was sur-
rounded by around six people, so he couldn't
have seen me anyway, even without the mask.

Paul skated up to us. "Anyone hurt?" he
asked.

"No," Tracie said. "He just has to be sure
nobody catches the measles from him."

"That's why he's wearing that thing," Nina
said.

"Hmm," Paul said. "I never heard of it being
used for that purpose. I thought it was to protect
against the cold."

"Oh, it'll do that too," I said. "It's good for a
lot of things."

"Can I get one, Daddy?" Tracie said. "I love
it."

"I think I have one at home from some skiing
venture," Paul said. "I'll see if I can dig it up. So,
everybody ready for a bit of cake and ice
cream?"

"Yeah!" all Tracie's friends yelled.

"Paul, I'd better be going," Mom said, touching his sleeve. "I had a wonderful time."

He leaned over and hugged her. "You were
terrific, El," he said. "You're a natural."

Mom smiled at him. I guess she likes him a lot.
I never saw her look at anybody that way.

"Let me help you with your skates," he said. He turned to the rest of us. "Let's start getting rounded up."

He and Mom skated off hand in hand.

Nina looked at me. "Your mother doesn't act that old or look that old," she said. "She seems nice."

"Yeah," I said.

"His last girl friend was the pits." She skated along next to me. "There was nowhere to go but up. He sure has weird taste in girl friends sometimes."

10

When we got to Paul's apartment, there was a clown there who let us in.

"Oh, hi," Paul said. "You got here okay?"

"Oh, yeah, everything was fine," the clown said. "Hi, Robbie! I didn't know you were coming."

The clown's voice sounded familiar, but I couldn't tell from where. It didn't look like anyone I knew. "Hi," I said, puzzled.

"It's me—Jill," she said as Tracie and her friends came in.

I never expected to see Dad's girl friend at Tracie's party. That was kind of strange. Then I remembered how she'd told Paul she was a clown and how she was looking for a job. Once I knew it was Jill, I could recognize her more. But she really looked completely different. Her face was all white, with a big red spot on the end of her nose, and she had big circles painted around her eyes. She had a ruffle around her neck and a pointed hat covered with silver stars.

"Are you supposed to be funny or do you do tricks?" Nina asked.

"I don't know," Jill said. "I guess—"

"Neens, why don't you let Ms. Klotz show us what she can do without having to run interference at the same time."

Tracie and some of her friends doubled over. "Klotz! Is that your *real* name?"

Jill tried to laugh. "Yeah, it—it's awful, isn't it? They used to call me The Klutz in school. I was so tall and everything."

"You don't seem exceptionally tall," Paul said, looking down at her.

"Nobody's as tall as you, Daddy," Tracie said. To her friends she said proudly, "He's six feet and four inches."

"I'm five eight," Jill said, "but I was that tall when I was twelve! All the boys came up to my shoulder. Nobody'd ever ask me to dance or anything. I really *was* a klutz."

I hope I'm not too short when I grow up. Neither of my parents is particularly tall. I know not all girls mind, but I think most of them want you to be taller than they are. Penny's taller than me already and Eve almost is. I take vitamins every morning, but it doesn't seem to have done that much good so far.

"Thank God we all grow out of our adolescent

identities," Paul said. To Jill he said, "Are you all set up?"

"Sure."

She had put all her stuff on this table in the middle of the room that was covered with a long cloth. There were some things on the table: cards, flowers, a newspaper. First she did the magic tricks. They were really easy ones. Thor's older brother, Derek, has this book on card tricks, and these were ones right from the beginning of the book. I mean *I* could've done them, they were that easy. But Tracie and her friends seemed impressed. I guess ten-year-old girls are pretty easy to fool.

Jill cleared her throat. She reached down to the floor and took a rabbit out of a cage. "Uh, this is Sylvester," she said.

"Hi, Sylvester," one of Tracie's friends said.

"Can we pet him?" Tracie asked.

"Later," Jill said. "Okay? He might get nervous."

"Is he your rabbit?" Nina asked.

"I rent him from this place," Jill said. She smiled at us uncertainly. "I'm going to make him disappear."

"Can you make him come back?" one of Tracie's friends asked in a worried voice. She was the one who had just watched while we skated.

"Sure," Jill said. "He's always come back before."

"She's not going to make him disappear," Nina said in this voice like a teacher. "She's going to make it seem like he disappears. It's a trick."

"Oh," the girl said. But she still looked worried.

Jill took this big multicolored scarf and began waving it back and forth in front of the rabbit. Then she whipped it to one side. Just as she did that, there was this loud thunk. When she took the scarf away, the rabbit wasn't there.

You could tell the rabbit had fallen through a hole in the table. That was what that thunk was. I didn't say anything because, like I say, maybe they were all fooled. Then there was this faint squeaking noise.

"I think he's hurt," Nina said.

"Who?" said Tracie.

"The rabbit! I think he fell through a hole and got hurt."

Jill began looking worried.

"He didn't fall through a *hole*," Tracie said. "He disappeared."

"Sure he fell through a hole," Nina said. "What do you think's making that squeaking noise?"

We all were quiet.

"Yeah, I hear it," Tracie said softly. To Jill she said, "Did he really fall through a hole?"

Jill nodded sadly. "He must've fallen the wrong way," she said.

Everyone came up to the table. Jill slid the part of the table under the cloth to one side. Down in there, in a kind of box, was the rabbit. Jill took him out. "Gee, I hope he's okay," she whispered.

I took the rabbit from her. We had a pet rabbit once at school and I was the one who took care of him, so I know quite a lot about rabbits, more than most people my age. "I think he might have hurt his foot," I said.

"Oh, dear," Jill said.

"Daddy!" Nina yelled. "The rabbit's hurt!"

Paul came in. He'd been in the kitchen. He was wearing a chef's hat, which made him look even taller.

"He was supposed to disappear," Tracie said, "but he fell instead."

Paul began feeling the rabbit gently all over. He looked at Jill. "I think he's okay."

"Are you sure?" Jill started to cry. "I'm so worried."

Paul handed the rabbit to me again. "Yes," he said in a soothing voice, patting Jill on the shoulder. "He'll be fine. He's just had a little shock, that's all. . . . Let's give him a little lettuce and a carrot or two."

"I'm sorry," Jill said. "Should I leave now? I really made a mess out of everything."

"Leave without cake?" Paul said. "And here I've been slaving for three days over this cake.

84

Well, if you want to wound me to the core . . ."

"I like cake," Jill said, sniffing. She wiped her eyes.

"Those were good tricks," Tracie said. "Would you teach me how to do them?"

"Sure, maybe some other time," Jill said.

"I can do some too," I said.

"I think I want to be a clown when I grow up," Tracie said. "Only I want to be the kind in the circus that comes out of a little car."

Paul had made a great birthday cake. It had three layers, with the smallest on top, and real flowers sticking out all over it. Everyone stood around looking at it after Tracie blew out the candles.

"Gee, that's the prettiest cake I ever *saw*," Jill said. She'd taken all her clown makeup off. She looked the way she usually does. "Maybe we shouldn't eat it."

Paul was going around taking pictures of everything with a Polaroid camera. "It has to be eaten," he said. He took the flowers off the cake and gave one to each of the girls. Jill put one in her hair.

After the cake Tracie opened her presents. She got some books and a record and some other stuff like jewelry. I gave her a game I like that my uncle gave me last Christmas. I hoped she didn't have it already. Tracie seemed to like everything she got. Every time she opened something, she said, "Wow!" and passed it around to show everyone.

Then they had some games. I won the Chess Challenger game. I had been practicing, playing with Dad. "Here's your prize," Tracie said.

The prize was this very small chess set. "You can play with it on trains and buses," Tracie said. "That's what it says."

The trouble is, I don't take trains that frequently, and I usually don't spend enough time on a bus to play a whole game of chess. Maybe one move or two. "Thanks," I said.

"Now let's play the record," Tracie said, "and we can dance."

"Who're we supposed to dance with?" one of her friends said. "There's only *him*." She pointed at me like I couldn't see her.

"So we can all dance with him," Tracie said. "Only me first, because it's my party."

"We can dance with each other," another of her friends said. "Who says you can only dance with a boy?"

First I got scared. Then I decided to pretend I knew how to dance. I figured it couldn't be worse than roller-skating. Paul put on the record. "Who will do me the honor?" he said, coming over to Tracie's friends. They all began to giggle. He picked the girl who was worried about the rabbit. They really looked funny dancing together since he was so much taller than her. He still had his chef's hat on.

You want to know something? Dancing wasn't bad. I did okay, especially considering I never did it before and didn't know what I was doing. Of course, they didn't know either. Dancing with someone who knew how might be harder.

"Do you have a girl friend?" Tracie asked, panting. At the end of her braid she had a barrette shaped like a pair of lips that looked like they were opening and closing.

"Um." I thought. "In a way."

"In what way?"

"Well, she's this girl in my class at school." I didn't want to tell her about the getting married thing.

"Oh, well, that's okay," Tracie said. Every time she moved, her braid swung back and forth. "You can have one *in* school and one *out* of school. I'll be your one out of school."

She seemed to regard it as settled. Boy, here I have two girl friends and I didn't even do anything to get them. I better be careful or I'll end up with a hundred of them. Still, look at Thor—he has two at camp and three at school and one just in his building. I guess it's not so bad. I'd never tell anyone I had a girl friend who was ten years old, though.

I had to dance with all of Tracie's friends. One of them was a lot taller than me, but most of them

87

were my size or shorter. When I got done with all of them, I looked at Nina.

"You don't have to," she said. She was sitting at the table, eating some more cake.

"Don't you want to?"

"Sure, why not?" she said. She stood up. "I'm awful. I have no sense of coordination."

"I never even did it before," I told her.

"Really?" She looked surprised. "But you're good at sports. . . . You're more of a body person. There are head people and body people. I'm strictly a head person."

I never thought of that before. It's funny to think of some people with all bodies and tiny little heads and some with big huge heads and almost no bodies.

"Looks like your mother has some competition," Nina said. She pointed off to the end of the loft. Paul and Jill were dancing together. They were dancing close like they do in the movies. He didn't have his chef's hat on anymore.

"I think maybe my father might not like that," I said.

"How come?"

"She's his girl friend. She lives with him."

"That one?"

"Yeah."

"Oh, wow."

We looked over at them again. They just kept dancing around in a circle.

"Oh, boy." Nina sighed. "Are we going to get stuck with *her* now?"

"I think she likes my father," I said carefully. "At least she always acted like she did."

"Better not tell him."

I shook my head.

After the dancing Jill said she had to go home. "We can share a cab, Robbie," she said, "if you want."

"Let me help you with all your stuff," Paul said. He carried the table downstairs, Jill carried a shopping bag with her equipment, and I carried the cage with the rabbit. The rabbit seemed okay.

"Better have him checked over," Paul said. He looked outside the front door of the building. It was raining.

"I will," Jill said. A cab pulled up in front of us. "Well, thanks for such a lovely afternoon," she said. "I'm really sorry I goofed everything up."

"You were sensational," he said. "Thanks for coming, Robbie. You were a big help too."

We got into the cab. Paul handed the rabbit's cage in to me.

"Good-bye!" Jill called as the cab pulled off. "Good-bye!" She looked out the back window at Paul. I turned around and looked too. He just stood there in the rain, watching us, till we pulled out of sight.

11

One trouble with Thor's family having a country house is he can hardly ever stay over with me in the city. Their house is about three hours away from New York and they go there practically every weekend, even in the winter. But this one weekend in April they didn't go because his mother was sick. So he said he could stay over at my house Saturday.

Mom said that was okay. She said she and Paul were going to the movies. Thor came over around five. He said he had something to show me. He'd told me about it on the phone. He made it sound like a big deal.

What it was, was these photos of his brother's girl friend with no clothes on. His brother wants to be a photographer, and he has a darkroom in their apartment, so he develops all his own pictures. Thor took them out of the bag. They were kind of weird. His brother's girl friend looked a little like what Eve might look like if she doesn't get too fat and gets to have a really good figure. What I mean is, she had blond hair and the kind of eyes Eve has that are far apart. He took her picture in these really strange poses. There was a whole bunch where she was holding a sword, and some others where she was eating a bunch of grapes.

"What's the sword for?" I asked.

"I don't know," Thor said. "He collects them. I guess it's just to have a pose or something. She can't just be lying there."

"What if he looks for these pictures and they're not there? Won't he get mad?"

"He's away this weekend." Thor leaned over my shoulder. "What's funny is with clothes *on* she doesn't look that great. Her personality isn't that sexy."

"Yeah."

"What do you mean, yeah? You never saw her!"

"I just mean I can imagine that."

"Did you see Eve that way yet?"

I shook my head. "We're not married any-more—she said she didn't want to be." After a second I added, "She said she just wanted to be my girl friend."

91

"Great!" Thor said. "That's a cinch, then. Tell her you don't have a sister and you wonder what girls look like without clothes."

"I know what they look like."

"Everybody knows what they look like. But it's a good excuse."

Mom fixed us some hamburgers. She was in a bathrobe and it looked like she had just washed her hair. "I haven't seen you in such a long time, Thor," she said. "How've you been?"

"Okay," Thor said. He thinks my mother makes the best hamburgers he ever tasted. I don't personally see how they're that different from any other ones. "Boy, these are great hamburgers, Mrs. Post." He always says that.

Mom beamed.

Later Paul came to pick Mom up. He acted friendly to me, like always. "Been practicing your dancing, Robbie?" he said, smiling.

"Dancing?" Mom said, surprised. Thor looked at me the same way. I turned red.

"Listen, he had them lined up all afternoon. A weaker man would have begged off."

"At the party?" Mom said. "You never mentioned that, Robbie."

I didn't say anything.

Paul said, "We better get a move on, El—there may be a line."

Mom bent down and kissed me. "Have fun, boys."

After they left, Thor said, "What party was that?" Usually we go to parties together since they're given by kids in our class.

"Oh, it was just this party," I said.

"What girls was he talking about?"

"Just some girls." I decided not to tell him they were ten years old. "He has a daughter. It was her party."

"Your mother's boyfriend?"

"Yeah."

"She going to marry him?"

I shrugged. I thought of the party and of Paul and Jill dancing. But the next week, when I stayed with Dad, she was still there.

"Listen, I have a great idea," Thor said.

"What?"

"Let's go see *The Empire Strikes Back*."

"Now?"

"Yeah, it's supposed to be terrific."

"I know, but Mom would never let me go out at night without a grown-up."

"So? We'll be back before they will. Anyhow, it's right in our neighborhood. It's safe."

I thought about it. I really had wanted to see *The Empire Strikes Back* for a long time. And it wasn't the kind of movie Mom would ever go to. She mostly goes to foreign movies. "Do you have money?"

"Enough."

We figured if we went to the eight-o'clock

show, we'd be back by around ten. Mom never comes back until at least twelve when she goes out on dates, sometimes later. Sometimes I go to bed at twelve and she's *still* not home. I don't like that so much. I like someone to be in the house when I fall asleep. If she's not back, I put the light on in the hall and keep my door open. If she's back, I shut it.

There was a line. Thor got on the end of it and I went to get the tickets. As I was going back to the end of the line, all of a sudden I saw Dad and Jill. Dad likes science fiction so it made sense that he might want to see *The Empire Strikes Back*. Still, I was hoping he wouldn't see me. But just as I passed them Jill called out, "Hi, Robbie!"

I swallowed. "Hi."

"Robbie," Dad said, "what're you doing here?"

"Well, um, Thor and me are seeing the movie."

Dad isn't as strict as Mom about most things. He looked slightly puzzled. "Didn't you see it already?"

"Uh-uh." Then I realized he might think we were there with Mom! "I better get at the end of the line," I said. "See you."

Dad smokes, so he would go to the smoking section. That meant if Thor and I could sit near the back, we could get out right when it ended and Dad didn't have to find out we weren't with Mom.

94

The movie was great, but I won't go into that, because if you've seen it, you know and if you haven't, I don't want to spoil it for you. Just as it ended I yanked on Thor's sleeve. "Quick."

"Take it easy."

"I don't want them to see us."

We got up and started walking out. Just as we were almost out the door, I heard someone say, "Isn't that Robbie?"

It was Paul's voice. Then I heard Mom say, "Robbie!"

I froze.

"What are you two doing here?" Mom said. She looked bewildered more than anything.

"We just decided to see the movie," I said.

"Alone? At night?"

"Well, Dad's here. He wanted to see it." Suddenly I wanted Dad to appear more than anything.

"Oh, you're here with Roger." She looked relieved. "Where is he?"

"He sat in the smoking section," I said. I could see Thor looking at me with admiration for my quick thinking.

A couple of minutes later Dad and Jill walked out. "Ellen," Dad said, taken aback. "Hello . . . I didn't think this was your kind of thing."

"Well, there was such a line for *La Cage aux Folles*. And it wasn't bad, really."

"I *loved* it," Jill sighed.

There was a pause.

"Say, I know a great ice-cream place near here," Paul said. "How does that strike everybody?"

"Great!" Thor said. He's an ice-cream freak. Actually, I don't think Paul was asking *him* so much, but everyone else seemed to think it was a good idea too.

This place Paul knew about really did have great ice cream. Thor and I ordered a banana split, which was gigantic—about eight scoops of ice cream and all kinds of junk poured over it. Whenever I go into an ice-cream place, I'm glad I'm skinny. The grown-ups all just had coffee or sodas except for Jill, who got a chocolate-marshmallow cone.

"So, how's the rabbit?" Paul asked. He and Mom and I were sitting on one side, Thor was at the end, and Dad and Jill were on the other side.

"Oh, he's fine," Jill said. She licked her cone and looked from Mom to Dad. "I had this rabbit. For my act? I rent him. I make him disappear—well, really, he just goes through this hole in the table, but this time he kind of fell, and I was afraid he sprained his ankle. But it turned out he was okay."

Mom took a sip of her coffee. "I think I'm a little lost," she said. "Where did all this take place?"

96

"At Tracie's party," Paul said. "Jill did some magic tricks, and the rabbit was part of the act."

Jill turned to Mom. "See, I put up these signs all over the West Side, about how I could do shows for children, like at parties? But nobody called. . . . And then here I had my chance and I messed up. I was_terrible!"

"You were terrific," Paul said. "All Tracie can talk about now is how she wants to be a clown."

"Really?" Jill said, looking pleased. She had a blob of ice cream on the end of her nose, but I don't think she knew it.

Paul nodded. "You have a real comic gift," he said. "Did you study mime?"

"Yeah." She frowned. "It's hard to be funny on purpose. Sometimes you are without meaning to, but that doesn't count."

"Sure it counts," Paul said. "Everything counts."

"It's not a way to make a living," Jill rushed on. "It's not a real job, but it feels good, you know? Making people laugh."

"Have you ever thought of joining the circus?" Mom said.

"Well . . ." Jill looked uncertain. "You'd have to travel a lot and it wouldn't be, like, a normal life. I want a normal life. I mean, not right now necessarily, but eventually. You know, like children and a home and things like that?"

"Yes," Mom said. "I know."

"You'll get them, then," Paul said. "Everybody gets what they want in life . . . sooner or later."

"They do?" Dad said.

"Basically."

"A comforting thought," Dad said. "I'd like to believe that."

When we got out of the ice-cream place, Mom and Paul said they were going to take us home in a cab. Dad and Jill said they wanted to walk. I'd been scared Mom would say something to Dad like "Thanks for taking Robbie to the movies," but she didn't.

When we got home, Mom said Thor and I had to go straight to bed. It was pretty late, nearly twelve.

"Your father's girl friend is really pretty," Thor said as we got into our pajamas."

"Yeah."

"I like girls with long blond hair. That's the kind I'm going to marry—are you?"

"I don't know." I guess I don't care that much what color hair girls have.

Thor fell right to sleep, but I stayed awake, I don't know why. I could hear Mom and Paul talking in her bedroom.

"I just wondered why you never mentioned it," she was saying. She sounded angry.

"It didn't seem important," Paul said. "She

just mentioned she did it and I thought— Look, magicians cost an arm and a leg. She was a real bargain."

"Yes, I can imagine," Mom said. "I imagine her rates are quite reasonable."

Eventually I heard the front door slam. Then the house was quiet.

12

Our spring vacation was in April, during a week I stayed with Dad. When I got there, Jill wasn't there. I figured maybe she finally got a job. But when Dad came home, he said she wasn't living there anymore. He stood there, looking awkward.

"She needed—well, time to think things over," he said.

"Sure," I said.

"She's very young and . . ."

I couldn't tell if he minded or not. It's hard to tell things like that with my father. "So," he said with a smile, "it'll be the two of us, just like old times."

I wasn't sure what old times he meant. I guess he meant before Jill moved in.

He started cooking supper. "Just two old bachelors fending for themselves," he said.

Actually my father isn't a bad cook. He doesn't have a whole lot of things he cooks, but some of them are pretty good. He makes this chicken dish sometimes that's terrific. He said he learned it in college. "You liked Jill, didn't you, Robbie?" he said, putting the food down in front of me.

"Sure," I said. "She was okay."

"The funny thing," he said, "is I lived alone and loved it till I met Ellen, but since then . . . You get used to living with someone, and then you miss it."

"Can I eat with my hands?" I said. Dad usually lets me do that with chicken.

"You need someone to talk to at night," Dad said, "or just to listen, just to care. Women are good at listening."

I began gnawing on the drumstick.

"So how's *your* social life, Robbie?" Dad said. "Any new conquests?"

"Nothing special."

"Jill said what's-his-name's little daughter was quite taken with you."

"She's only ten," I explained.

"Hang in there. Before you know it, she'll be thirteen."

Before I know it? Three *years!*

"It's practice for the real thing," he said, drinking some wine.

"What is?"

101

"Girls, that whole thing. You have to practice."

"You mean to get good at it?" I said.

"Well, not good. . . . Just finding out what it's like, *and* what you're like."

"I know what I'm like," I said, not sure what he was talking about. My father is like that. Sometimes it's hard to know exactly what he's talking about.

Dad smiled at me. "You'll do okay," he said. "I'm not worried about you at all. You're not the way I was at your age."

"What were you like?" It's hard to imagine Dad at my age, though I've seen photos of him. He was skinny, like me, but he had glasses.

"I was hopeless," Dad said. "Shy, rotten at sports. I never knew what to say to girls. I used to write down topics on pieces of paper and memorize them, and then forget everything I'd written down." He smiled.

"I'm a little bit like that," I said.

"You're not as bad as me," Dad insisted. "Believe me. Nobody wanted to marry *me* when I was eleven."

I wanted to explain to him that getting married hadn't been the way he thought. I don't even know if it meant Eve liked me that much. She might have just figured everyone was doing it so why not her, and I just happened to be standing there.

Saturday we went to the park and did a lot of stuff together. It was kind of more fun without Jill, but I didn't tell Dad that. When we got home, it was dinnertime again. I wondered what specialty Dad was going to fix this time.

"Robbie, tonight I'm going out with a friend," he said. "Is that okay? I thought since we spent so much time together today . . ."

"Sure," I said.

Dad fixed me this other specialty of his, salami and eggs. It's not bad if you pour a lot of ketchup over it and eat a lot of French fries at the same time. "Her name's Marilyn," he said.

I just nodded. My mouth was full.

"She'll come over for a drink and then we'll go out," Dad said. "She's an old friend of Ellen's and mine."

She didn't look that old. She looked more about Mom's age.

"Why, hi, Robbie," she said. She came into Dad's living room. He gave her a drink of something. "Haven't *you* changed!"

"He got married," Dad said. "Marriage does that to a man."

"Dad, come on." What a dumb thing to say!

Marilyn kept looking around the living room. "I *love* what you've done with the place," she said. "It looks marvelous, Roger."

"I like the apartments in this building," Dad said. He was drinking something too.

103

"And it isn't awkward with—" She stopped. "How's your mother?" she said to me.

"Okay."

Marilyn sank back onto the couch. "I have a little girl just your age—Sandra. We must get you together some time."

"It's fine by me," Dad said, "but Robbie here has a pretty full schedule. He has girls coming out of his ears."

I just looked at him. If you never met my father, you'd think he was a real idiot, judging by the dumb things he was saying. Only he's not.

"Sandra is very shy," Marilyn said. "I think she's a little afraid of boys." She laughed. "Do you like shy girls, Robbie?"

I shrugged.

"He's a man of catholic tastes," Dad said. "Like his father." He stood up. "Well! Shall we . . . ?"

I think my father still doesn't know how to act with women, if you want my opinion. I guess he isn't that different from when he was my age. I never heard him say so many stupid things in a row. When he had left, I realized one bad thing. He still hadn't gotten his TV fixed and there was this great movie on TV. I decided to call Mom and see if she'd mind if I came over and borrowed her TV. If she was out, I could just go over and borrow it and return it when the show was over. But she hadn't gone out.

104

"What's up, hon?" she said.

I asked her about the TV.

"Stay put, I'll bring it over," Mom said.

We just have a little TV, a twelve-inch one, but you get really good reception on it, even without a cable.

"Can I watch it with you?" Mom said. "I've heard it's pretty good." She plugged the TV into an outlet in the living room. "Where's Roger?"

"He went out," I said.

"With Mousie?"

I shook my head. "She moved out."

Mom looked surprised. "Since when?"

"I don't know. She wasn't here when I came. Dad said—" Then I stopped. I couldn't remember exactly what he said.

"What?" Mom said.

"I forget. . . . That she's young."

"Yeah," Mom said. "True enough."

"He said she needed time to think things over."

Suddenly Mom burst out laughing. "Maybe she joined the circus!"

"I don't think so, Mom."

She simmered down. "Who *did* he go out with?"

"Someone named Marilyn."

"God, not Marilyn Sussman!"

I shrugged.

Mom sighed. "He must be really desperate. . .

Did she have straight black hair with bangs down to her eyes?"

"I guess, kind of. I can't remember."

"Oh, dear, poor Roger."

The movie was good. In the middle we had ice cream and cookies. I was glad Mom had come over. It's not that I mind being by myself, but it's more fun watching a movie with someone else. Just as it was over and they were going into the eleven-o'clock news, the door opened. It was Dad and Marilyn.

"Oh . . . hi, Ellen," Dad said.

"Robbie wanted to watch something on TV," Mom said quickly, "so I brought the set over. Yours still isn't fixed?"

"I guess I should attend to that," Dad said, "but . . ."

"Hi, Ellen," Marilyn said. "Gee, I love your hair! When did you get it done?"

"Oh, I've had it this way for months," Mom said, touching her hair. "Some days I wake up looking like I've been electrocuted, but it's easy. It doesn't have to be set or anything."

"I wish I had the courage," Marilyn said.

There was a pause.

"How's your job?" Mom said.

"Busy, busy, hectic . . . what can I tell you?"

Mom jumped up. "Listen, why doesn't Robbie come back with me tonight? There was something we were thinking of doing tomorrow."

That was news to me.

"That's fine with me," Dad said eagerly. "If he wants—"

"Okay," I said.

Mom picked up the TV.

"Can you manage?" Dad said.

"Sure," Mom said. "It's not heavy. . . . Nice to see you again, Marilyn."

Marilyn smiled.

We walked across the lobby.

"Is she the one you thought?" I asked Mom.

Mom nodded. "Yup, the very same."

I got right into bed when I got upstairs, but I couldn't fall asleep. Maybe it was that I was supposed to be with Dad but was here instead. It made me feel mixed up. Then I heard this sound. At first I didn't know what it was. Then I realized it was Mom, crying.

I went into her bedroom. She was lying there with her face in the pillow. "Mom?"

She looked up. Her eyes were all red. "Oh, honey! I'm sorry."

"Are you okay?"

"I just—I just feel so bad!" She started to cry again.

I didn't know what to do. I went over to her. "Would you like something to eat?"

She shook her head. Then she sat up. "I'm

okay, hon, really. I just feel lonely sometimes." She lay back again, not crying, but just lying there.

"I could read you this story," I said. "It's pretty good. . . . Do you want me to?"

"Sure," she said softly. "I'd like that."

The story was in this science fiction magazine, *Omni*, that Dad gets. I'd already read the first page, but I read it again for her. It was really an interesting story, about this country where the people don't have any sense of time. I looked up at Mom once in a while while I was reading. She was lying back, staring off into space. I couldn't tell if she was listening or not. When I looked over at her again, her eyes were closed and she was breathing evenly. "Mom, are you asleep?"

Since she didn't answer, I figured she was. I went over and clicked off the light. Then I covered her with her blanket and went back to my room. I decided to finish the story in the morning.

13

"We have a surprise today, class," Ms. McBride said. "This is Mr. Nimmo. He's the drama teacher for the high school. This spring the senior class is performing a play called *The Castle of Bora*, which was written by one of our seniors. It's a play about a royal family who lived in the Middle East, and Mr. Nimmo is here because he needs a baby for the play. . . . Would you like to explain what you're looking for, Mr. Nimmo?"

Mr. Nimmo was a short guy with a beard. "Right," he said. "Well, it's not a big part. But we need a baby who can keep his cool onstage. Not all babies can. We could use a doll, but we figured a real baby would be more impressive."

"What lines does he have?" Penny asked.

Mr. Nimmo smiled. "There won't be any actual lines," he said, "but he has to have a royal presence."

109

"Does it have to be a boy?" Eve asked. She and Penny are a team in our Child Care class. They have a girl baby named Theodora.

"No, it doesn't have to be a boy," Mr. Nimmo said. "The baby in the play *is* a boy, but I doubt that at this age anyone could tell the difference."

"Now, class," Ms. McBride said. "If your baby is selected, you'll have to participate in the play. Mr. Nimmo thought that since you've been working with these babies for several months, your presence would make them feel at home."

"Will *we* get to be in the play?" I asked. I'm not sure I'd like that so much, especially if I had to memorize a lot of lines.

"Not actually *in* the play," Mr. Nimmo said, "but you'll be backstage and you'll have a chance to watch rehearsals."

"Will we miss classes?" Patrick said.

"No," Ms. McBride said quickly. "Absolutely not. . . . All right, now, please *only* volunteer if you and your partner are willing to see this project through to the end."

I looked at Thor. "I guess we might as well."

"Sure. Tig would be great. How about it, Tiger? You want to make your debut?"

Tigran looked at Thor. "Ta," he said.

We think that's his way of saying "Thor," but it's hard to tell. He calls me "Ro."

"Let's see a show of hands," Ms. McBride said. "Thor, I said put up your *hand*, not your

110

baby." Thor was holding Tigran up over his head so Mr. Nimmo could see him. A lot of kids had their hands up. "Well, you see, we have a lot of interest," she said to Mr. Nimmo. "This is a very responsive class."

Mr. Nimmo told us he would go around the room and look at each baby. "I'd like you to tell me why you think *your* baby would do a good job," he said.

I looked at Thor. "What should we say?" I muttered.

"We'll figure something out," he said.

We just kind of played around with Tigran while Mr. Nimmo went around the room. I heard Penny saying, "Our baby is very smart. She knows twenty-five words. She can repeat things you tell her. Say Nimmo, Theodora."

"Nimmo," Theodora said.

"Boy, I bet Tigran couldn't do that," I whispered to Thor. "He'd probably just say 'Nuh.' "

Finally Mr. Nimmo came around to us. He looked down at Tigran. "Quite a head of hair," he said, seeming impressed.

"Yeah, well, that's one reason we thought Tiger here would be good," Thor said quickly. "Because onstage a bald baby would be kind of . . . not so great. Black hair stands out."

"His name is Tiger?" Mr. Nimmo said.

"That's not his real name," I said. "His real name is Tigran. He's named after an Armenian

111

king named Tigran the Great. He's from the Middle East." Actually I think it's Tigran's parents who are from the Middle East—he was born in Paris—but it sounded good.

"Would you say he's a good-natured baby?" Mr. Nimmo asked. "Easy to handle?"

"Oh, sure," Thor said. "He's a cinch—he'll laugh at anything. Go on, do your monster act, Robbie."

I bent down and bared my teeth. Tigran roared with laughter. It's funny. He'd seen me do that about fifty times, but he still seemed to get a big bang out of it.

"Tigran the Great, huh?" Mr. Nimmo said thoughtfully, looking at Tigran.

Tigran reached out and touched Mr. Nimmo's beard.

At the end of the class Mr. Nimmo announced that he'd made his decision. "I don't want any of you to think that if your baby wasn't picked, it's any reflection on his or her looks or abilities. This is a really impressive bunch of babies. . . . But I think for our particular play this hairy young fellow in the back, Tigran, is just what we need."

"Yay, Tiger!" Thor said. He held Tigran up like he'd just won him at a fair.

"Thor, quiet, please," Ms. McBride said.

"I'll let the two of you know about rehearsals," Mr. Nimmo said. "I'm sure we'll have a good working relationship."

112

Eve came over to look at Tigran. "How come they chose *him?*" she said, sounding sad.

"Because he's the best," I said, grinning.

"He's not even smart," Penny said. "He hardly even talks."

"Yeah, but he's descended from royalty," Thor said. "He's the real McCoy."

"Thor, come *on* . . . you *know* that's not true. That's just his name. Probably in Armenia it's a really common name, like Joshua."

"You never can tell," he said.

"I think he just picked him because he has hair," Eve said. "It does make him look older."

"Well, *I* think it's prejudiced," Penny said. "They said it didn't have to be a boy and then they went ahead and picked a boy anyway." She marched off, looking mad.

Thor and I smiled at each other. We started stuffing Tigran into his coat. We're supposed to have them all ready when the mothers come. "We ought to give him a prize," I said, "for beating out all the other babies."

Thor looked in his pockets. He took out some chocolate. "Here, Tig . . . gobble up, boy."

Tiger gobbled up the chocolate right away.

When his mother came to pick him up, we told her about it.

"Mr. Nimmo thought he was the best?" she said, looking pleased. "My Tigran?"

"Yeah," I said. "He did." Actually it hadn't so

113

much been being the best, but maybe thinking that made her feel good.

"He won't have any lines or anything," Thor said. "You don't have to worry about that."

"Lines?" She looked puzzled.

"He means Tig—Tigran won't have to say anything in the play," I said. "Someone'll just carry him around and stuff like that."

"And we'll be right there to kind of look after him," Thor said. "If they want him to laugh, Rob here'll just do his monster face. Show her, Rob."

I felt pretty funny doing the face in front of Tigran's mother, but I did. He laughed, as usual. Mrs. Lambert laughed too. "You're an actor!" she said.

"Not really," I said. "I can just make funny faces."

"His face is funny even when he doesn't make faces," Thor said. "He's just got that kind of face."

I socked him.

Mrs. Lambert took Tigran up in her arms. "You boys will make good fathers someday. You like babies, no?"

Thor and I looked at each other.

"Sure, they're okay," I said. "We like them pretty much."

After she left, Thor said, "I don't know if I like them especially."

I looked at him. "So, what're you going to

114

say? You hate them? . . . Don't you like Tig?"

"Yeah, but he's different—he's more like a real person. Maybe a boy wouldn't be so bad. But I sure wouldn't want to spend a lot of time changing diapers and stuff. Ugh!"

"My father did it," I said, "for me. He said it wasn't so bad."

"Pee-yoo," Thor said, holding his nose.

When I got home, Mom wasn't back yet. I went into the living room to watch TV a little before she came back. They had some after-school special on till five. I knew I couldn't watch till the end because I didn't want her to catch me watching. I timed it perfectly. I turned it off at 4:15 and she came home at 4:25.

"Hi, sweetie," Mom said. "How're things?"

"Okay."

"Were there any calls for me?"

I shook my head. I went into the kitchen with her. I told her about how Tigran had gotten picked for the play. "I think they might've just picked him because he has hair," I admitted.

"You were just like that," Mom exclaimed. "You had so much hair! Even before I brought you home from the hospital. The nurses couldn't get over it. . . . There was this mother I used to meet in the park, and she had a little girl who didn't have *one* hair on her head till she was two! Everyone thought she was a boy."

"Was I smart?" I asked.

Mom frowned. "What do you mean, hon?"

"Well, like in our class Penny and Eve have this baby who knows about twenty words already and Tig doesn't know any!"

"Oh, none of that matters," Mom said. "A couple of years later it all evens out." She went into the next room and came back with a manila envelope. She opened it up and dumped a whole pile of photos out on the dining-room table. "This is you when you were one," she said, showing me.

I looked at the photo. It's interesting. I did look a little like Tigran. My hair wasn't so black, though, and I didn't have such big eyes. I was sitting at the top of a slide and some other baby was sliding down.

"Who's that?" I asked.

"That was that little girl, the one without hair. What was her name? Anissa, I think. . . . She had such a crush on you! If we didn't go to the playground, her mother said she'd just sit in her carriage and not budge."

It's funny how you can't remember stuff like that at all, not even a little bit. I looked through some of the other photos. There were a bunch of Mom and Dad and me together at the beach. "Who took those?"

"Oh, a friend of ours," Mom said, looking over my shoulder. "That was your first summer. We rented a house on Fire Island."

116

It's hard to imagine that there was a time when my parents liked each other so much, the way they looked like they did in those photos. They were laughing and my father had his arm around my mother. In one picture she was kind of sitting in his lap while she held me.

Mom sighed. "That was a nice summer," she said.

"Yeah," I said. I couldn't remember anything about it, but it looked from the photos like it was. "You and Dad were really getting along then, weren't you?"

Mom reached down and hugged me. "We were, sweetie. . . . I wish it had lasted."

Neither of us said anything for a couple of minutes. Then Mom said, "Should I leave them out? Do you want to look at them some more?"

I hesitated. "Maybe some other time," I said. "I have a lot of homework to do."

She scooped the photos up and put them back in the envelope.

14

"You want to stay at our place this weekend?"
Thor asked me.

"Aren't you going to the country?"

"Mom's driving Derek up to look at colleges."

"Sure," I said.

It was my week to stay with Mom, but she was
busy correcting final exams for these courses she
teaches. Her teaching ends in May and then she
doesn't have to teach again till the fall. But she
has work to do over the summer anyway, writing
papers and things like that. Sometimes she
teaches summer school.

When I got to Thor's, Derek's girl friend was
there. She was driving up to look at colleges with
them too. I stared at her, to see if she looked like
those photos. But she didn't that much. I guess
it's hard to tell what people will look like with
their clothes off if you see them with their clothes

on. She was wearing glasses and had her hair in a ponytail. She looked more like a secretary or someone who would type things than someone who would lie around in dumb poses with a bunch of grapes.

"She doesn't look at all the same," I told Thor after they'd left.

"Who?"

"Your brother's girl."

"The same as what?"

"The same as in those photos you showed me—you know, with the sword?"

"Oh, that wasn't her. That was Terry."

"But they look the same!"

"I thought you just said they didn't."

"They look sort of the same." Now I couldn't remember anymore. "They have the same color hair, sort of."

"Yeah, but Terry, well, she's much more— She had much more of a figure."

"Oh," I said.

"Did you see Eve that way yet?"

"Cut it out," I said, annoyed. "I'm not going to. I told you that already."

Thor raised his eyebrows. "Okay, calm down. . . . You're missing a great chance. You'll regret it."

"I will *not!*"

"Those Spanish girls are supposed to be hot stuff."

"Thor, shut up, okay? She's not even Spanish. Her father just works down there."

"It's your loss."

I sat there a minute. "Anyway, wasn't it embarrassing?" I said.

"What?"

"When you did it that time with Penny."

He shook his head. "No, not especially."

I know it would be for me! "Well, I'm *not* going to do it with Eve. Definitely."

"Nobody's forcing you. . . . Look, I probably wouldn't have done it with Penny except she suggested it."

I don't know *what* I'll do if Eve suggests it. But she won't. Because she doesn't come over to my house or anything like that. And she doesn't have that kind of personality. Penny is more kind of bold. I'm really glad now I didn't trade Eve for Penny. At least Eve is sort of quiet and leaves me alone, pretty much, even at school.

Sunday morning we decided to walk around Greenwich Village. That's where Thor lives. We walked over to SoHo, which is a couple of blocks away from his building. Somehow it started looking familiar, and then I realized why. We were right near Paul Perrin's gallery. It was right there, across the street. In the window was this huge car made out of cereal boxes. Thor said, "Hey, look at that!"

120

"What?" I knew what he was looking at. Thor is crazy about cars.

"It's a whole car made out of cereal boxes! Wow!"

We went over to look at it. Inside the gallery were a lot of other cars and things, all made out of cereal boxes, big ones and little ones. "Boy, this is great. He must've had to eat a lot of cereal. I wish I'd saved all the cereal boxes I ever used. I could make this."

"Where would you put it?"

"I don't know. In my room."

"It'd take up your whole room."

"Let's go in," Thor said. "I want to see the rest of them."

We walked in. There were a few people strolling around, grown-ups. I didn't see Paul. But in the corner I saw Tracie and Nina. Tracie came over as soon as she saw us. She was wearing a blue terry-cloth thing with shorts. She had a friend with her, not one of the ones from the party.

"Hi, Robbie," she said. To her friend, she said, "Sabrina, this is my boyfriend, Robbie."

I turned red. Thor was standing right there. My boyfriend! "Uh . . . this is Thor," I said.

"What a weird name," Sabrina said, wrinkling her nose. She had braces.

"I am the God of Thunder," Thor said, raising

121

his hands up. He began making this weird sound he can make which sounds a little like real thunder.

Tracie and Sabrina began to giggle.

"I'm scared of thunder," Tracie said.

"Me too," Sabrina said. "Can you do lightning too?"

"Sure," Thor said. "When I'm in the mood."

Girls always like it when he does stuff like that.

Just then Paul walked in. He was with Jill. She was carrying a big bunch of pussy willows. They were laughing.

"Oh . . . hi, Robbie," he said when he saw me.

"Hi," I said. I couldn't figure out what Jill was doing there. She wasn't dressed like a clown, just regular, in jeans and a T-shirt.

"Look at these pussy willows," she said. "Aren't they wonderful?"

"They're pretty," Tracie said. She reached out and touched them. "They're so soft."

"They don't smell, though," Sabrina said. "They're not like real flowers."

"Yes, they do," Jill said seriously. "They smell."

They went off to find a vase for the pussy willows.

Thor looked at me. "Isn't she your father's—"

"Yeah," I said. I didn't want to talk about it.

Nina came over to me. "It's all your fault," she said.

"What?"

"Why'd you tell him about her? Now she's *living* with us."

"She *is?*"

"Yeah . . . and all she does is lie around all day, watching TV. She's worse than Tracie. She says she's 'between jobs.' " Nina rolled her eyes back.

"I know," I said.

Nina lowered her voice. "Listen, can't you get your father to take her back?"

"How?"

"Kidnap her or something."

"She's not a kid." I know you're not supposed to laugh at your own jokes, but I thought that was pretty funny. I laughed.

Nina just looked at me dolefully. "She's driving me crazy! . . . What happened to your mother?"

"What do you mean?"

"I thought he liked her."

I swallowed. I remembered Mom crying. "Well, she liked *him*," I said. "I know that."

We looked at each other.

"Look, ask your father if he'll take her back, okay? As a favor?"

"Okay," I said. "If you ask Paul about Mom."

"What should I ask?"

"If he still likes her."

"Okay . . . it's a deal." We shook hands on it.

Thor was roaming around looking at the cars. "This is the greatest thing I ever saw," he said, coming over.

"This is Nina," I said. To Nina I added, "He's the God of Thunder."

Nina raised her hands up. She made a sound like thunder. You know what? It sounded more like thunder than when Thor does it. I really cracked up. Thor just looked at her, surprised.

Tracie and her friend came running back. Tracie always seems to be running. I've hardly ever seen her stay still. "Jill's going to teach me how to be a clown," she said excitedly. "How to do the makeup and everything."

"Wow," Nina said.

"And I'm going to teach *her* to roller-skate," Tracie said. "It's a trade. Do *you* roller-skate?" she asked Thor.

He nodded. "I'm not too good, though."

"I can teach you," she said, "if you want. I taught Robbie."

"You did?" Thor said.

"First I have to learn to be a clown," she said. "I'm going to learn magic tricks and everything."

"*I* know magic tricks," Thor said.

Tracie's eyes widened. "You do?"

He grinned. "Sure. Pick a card, any card."

Just before we left, Nina took me aside and whispered, "Remember!"

"I will."

Outside on the street Thor said, "Wow, that's the prettiest girl I ever *saw*."

"Who?"

"That girl with the braid. . . . Is she a movie star?"

"Tracie? No, she's just a regular girl. She tried out for this musical, but she didn't get in."

"She's your girl friend?" He looked amazed.

I shrugged. "In a way."

"In a way! Boy, I guess there's a lot you don't tell me. And here I tell *you* everything."

"Well, she's only ten," I said.

"So?"

"She just *turned* ten. So she's more like nine than ten."

"Who cares? Don't you want her? *I'll* take her."

"No!" I said. "I like her."

"She taught you to roller-skate? What else did she teach you?"

Nothing. . . . Listen, it just happened because she was Mom's boyfriend's daughter." Then all of a sudden I felt awful. I remembered how Nina had said, "It's all your fault." And all of a sudden I realized it was. If it hadn't been for me, Paul and Jill never would've met. If I'd just said I'd stay with Uncle Peter that weekend! Now Mom was crying and Dad was miserable, and it was all because of me. It's true I didn't do it on purpose, but so what? I sure wrecked everything.

125

15

When I got home, Mom asked, "Did you have fun with Thor?"

"Yeah," I said. I didn't tell her about meeting Paul and Jill.

"I had a pretty good weekend," she said. "I started running."

I just nodded. My mother is not exactly the athletic type. Neither is my father.

"I figured, why not get in shape? And with the reservoir right there. I was really out of breath the first few times, but I think if I keep at it, that'll go away. I'm going to get up every morning at seven and do it. You can come too, Robbie, if you want, once school is over."

"Okay," I said.

I tried to figure out how to ask Dad about Jill, how to put it. I figured I'd better wait till Friday, when I saw him, even though I guess I could have asked him on the phone. But I'm not so good at talking to people on the phone.

Monday we had the first rehearsal for *The Castle of Bora*. It was really kind of a weird play. The girl who wrote it was a senior. Her name was Gerty McDonald. She had a round face with freckles. If you just saw her face, you might have thought she was a lot younger, especially since she was wearing overalls like little kids do.

"She might be really rich," Thor whispered to me.

"How come?" She didn't look that rich to me, more the opposite. Her sneakers had holes in them.

"Maybe her father owns McDonald's," he whispered back.

Sometimes Thor can be really dumb. There are probably hundreds of McDonald's in the Manhattan phone book alone!

I was holding Tigran on my lap. Mr. Nimmo said he should come to the first rehearsal just to get used to the stage and the other people who would be in the play. He was sucking his thumb and looking like he might fall asleep any minute. I hoped Gerty McDonald wouldn't take it personally.

She explained that the play would be like the Nativity story, the kind they tell at Christmas, but it would have modern touches and be funny. For instance, the three kings who came to present gifts to Mary, Joseph, and the baby would give them things like an electric blender, a bubble gum machine that lit up when you put a nickel in it, and a set of radio headphones that looked like Mickey Mouse ears. Joseph was supposed to put the headphones on and say, "Groovy, man. Thanks a lot."

Thor nudged me and made a face.

"It'll be okay," I said, though I kind of agreed.

Gerty had us run through a couple of the scenes without words. We handed Tigran over to this really pretty girl named Kim, who was playing Mary. She had the longest hair I ever saw. It was really black and shiny. If she'd wanted to, she could have sat on it. Tigran was asleep when I handed him to her.

She smiled at me. "He's cute," she said. "Is he your brother?"

"No," Thor said. He was standing next to me. "We just kind of look after him."

Gerty came over and looked at Tigran. His thumb was still in his mouth. He was making a sound like snoring. "He doesn't look like a very lively kid," she said with a worried expression.

"Oh, he's lively," Thor said. "Don't worry about that.

"Does he always make that noise?"

I shook my head. "Do you want us to wake him up?"

Gerty hesitated. "Well, I'd kind of like to see him in action, as it were."

I cleared my throat. "Hey, Tig, wake up," I said right near his ear.

He went right on sleeping. I looked at Thor.

You know what he did? Boy, is he dumb sometimes! He reached over and yanked Tigran's thumb out of his mouth. Tigran opened his eyes, looked around at everyone, and started to yell as loud as he could.

"I told you he's lively," Thor said.

Gerty sighed. "We need a lively, *cheerful* baby," she said. "This will never do."

"He's cheerful," Thor said. "Do your monster face, Rob."

I did my monster face. Tigran just stared at me. I did it some more. Finally he began to smile.

Gerty turned to Mr. Nimmo. "Yeah, but Robbie isn't going to be onstage," she said. "I want the kid to look like that onstage."

"I have an idea," Mr. Nimmo said. "Robbie can be one of the shepherds. His back can be to the audience. That way Robbie can make his monster face right in front of Tigran and no one in the audience will see."

Gerty's face lit up. "Terrific," she said. She hugged Mr. Nimmo. "You're a genius."

Mr. Nimmo looked pleased. "That okay with you, Robbie?"

129

"Sure, why not?" I looked at Thor. "How about my friend?"

"He can be one of the sheep," Gerty said. "We need a couple more sheep."

After we walked out, Thor looked really mad. "A sheep?" he said. "That's for little kids! What am I supposed to? Get down on all fours and baa?"

"Sure," I said cheerfully. "You'll be a smash."

"It's not fair." He kicked the side of the building.

"That's life," I said with a grin.

"This sounds like one of the dumbest plays anyone ever wrote," Thor said. "If I'd known it was going to be this dumb, I'd never have volunteered for Tigran to be in it."

"*You* were the one that yanked his thumb out, you jerk," I said. "You better not do that when he's about to go onstage!"

"I didn't know he sucked his thumb," Thor said. "He never did in class."

"Maybe he only does it when he's sleeping." I used to suck my thumb. I did it till I was seven, but I decided not to mention that.

"I never heard of a baby snoring," Thor said. "He sounded like my grandfather."

Tigran's mother was waiting in front of the building. "How did he do?" she asked with a big smile.

"Oh, he was great," I said.

130

"Uh." Thor looked at her a minute. "Does he, like, suck his thumb a lot?"

"Only when he sleeps," she said. "You will have no problem."

"No problem, huh?" Thor said as we walked off.

"Baaa," I said. I guess that was mean. I am glad I don't have to be a sheep, though.

16

Friday Dad made that same chicken dish again. While his back was turned, I said, "Dad . . . do you feel like taking Jill back?"

"Hmm?" Dad looked at me in that vague way he has, like he wasn't exactly listening.

I said it again.

"Jill? What do you mean?"

I began feeling nervous, like I wasn't doing it right. "I just thought you might want her back."

He smiled. "Why would I want her back?"

"I thought maybe you miss her."

Dad thought a moment. "Well, it's true, I do miss her at times, but . . . Let's see, how shall I put this? It's hard living with someone, Robbie."

"It is? What's so hard about it?"

"Well, another person has different ways of doing things, different things they want to do—"

"So how come people get married?" I said.

"People get married for a lot of strange reasons," Dad said. "Some good, some bad. Mostly they fall in love and they don't think about all of those things until it's too late."

"Oh," I said. "Like with you and Mom?"

"Well, no," Dad said. "Your mother and I got along rather well, but—" He stopped. "You know, Robbie, I'd like to talk to you about all of this, but I have the feeling it would make more sense to you when you're a little older."

"Okay," I said.

He stood there, gazing at me reflectively. "How did you happen to think about Jill?"

"I just . . . met her on the street."

"Oh." He looked interested. "Was she with someone?"

"No."

"Did she ask after me?"

I shook my head.

"She's a lovely girl—I'm very fond of her," Dad said. "But she's very"—he gestured vaguely—"drifting. She doesn't seem to know quite what she wants out of life."

I guess now she wants Paul Perrin, but I didn't say that. When you get to be my age, you know when to keep your mouth shut.

That night I called Nina. I waited for Dad to go out.

"It's me, Robbie," I said, in case she wouldn't know my voice.

"Oh, hi."

I swallowed. "Listen, it's not going to work."

"What'd he say?"

"He said he's very fond of her." I tried to think what else Dad had said. "But I got the feeling he doesn't want her back that much."

"So we're stuck with her, huh?"

"I guess. . . . What'd *your* father say?"

Nina hesitated. "Well, he said he thought your mother was a very nice person . . . but he's—ta da!—in love."

"With Jill?"

"Yeah."

"Is he going to marry her?"

"I hope not! He's been in love before, but now she's moved *in*, she's got all her stuff here." Nina sighed. "Maybe when I get back from camp, it'll be over. I hope so. I have to go to camp this year. I wasn't looking forward to it much, but now . . ."

"I'm going too," I said. "To some camp in Maine. You sleep in tents."

"Ours too," Nina said. "It sounds really sick. A lot of outdoor stuff. I had to go out and get a sleeping bag and a mess kit and things."

"I have to too. . . . They teach you how to build fires."

"What's the name of yours?"

"Triniwaha."

134

"Hey," Nina said. "That's weird. I think that's the boys' part of ours. It's across the lake."

I knew that. Patrick, the boy who married me and Eve, went there for two years, and he said they make you get together with the girls' camp for dances. "Well, at least we'll know each other," I said.

"Yeah. . . . Hey, listen, don't tell everybody I'm weird-looking and can't dance, okay?"

"Okay," I said. After a second I added, "You dance okay. You just need to practice."

"Maybe. . . . So anyhow, I'll see you. Thanks for asking your father. At least we tried."

"Sure."

I'm sort of glad Nina's going. It's better if you know at least one person. Maybe I should have said she wasn't that weird-looking. She isn't. She's not that pretty, but she's not weird.

I guess there's nothing I can do about the thing with Paul. If he's in love with Jill, that must mean he isn't in love with Mom. I don't think you can be in love with two people at the same time. I hope Mom isn't in love with him. She never said she was. But she acted kind of like she was, back at Tracie's party.

17

The rehearsals for *The Castle of Bora* went okay.
Sometimes Tigran fell asleep in the middle, but he
didn't snore as loudly as he had the first time.
Once Gerty looked at him.

"I hope this isn't the way the audience is going
to react," she said.

Thor looked really funny as a sheep. They had
the sheep wear those white suits with big blobs of
cotton glued on. Over their heads they wore
papier-mâché masks. I had to wear a thing like a
blue smock that came down to my ankles. I also
had to carry a cane, I guess to poke the sheep
with if they weren't moving fast enough.

Thor got kind of a crush on Kim, the girl who
was playing Mary, even though she was a senior
and had a boyfriend. "She has the prettiest hair
I've ever seen," he said.

"I thought you liked blondes," I reminded him.

"I think Tig likes her too," Thor
you, Tig? Is she your type, huh?"

Sometimes, when Tigran was sitti
lap, he would take a piece of her hai
around his finger. Once he started che
thought she'd really get mad, but
"He's adorable," she said.

"All he does is sit on her lap and he
star," Thor grumbled. "And I have to
on all fours and baa."

"Those are the breaks, pal," I said, p
with my cane. They call it a crook.

"Cut it out," Thor said. "So you're
herd! That's not such a big deal. Your b
the audience, anyway."

The performance was in school asser
the last day of school. I looked out at t
ence from backstage. It's not much of
actually, but for assemblies they hang a cu
front and put chairs out for everybody to
Our whole class was sitting off to one side.

I saw Mom, sitting right in the front rov
had said he would try to come too, but I
see him.

"There he is," Thor said. He had his cos
on, except for the sheep's head. "He's i
back."

I thought maybe Mom and Dad would wa
sit together. But maybe they each didn't k
the other was going to be at the play. Also,

't've wanted to sit near the back so he could
e quickly and not be too late for work.

sounds funny to say I was nervous when I
't have any lines, but I was. My heart started
ting really loudly. Tigran seemed fine. He
ked wide-awake. The only trouble was he
med hungry and we didn't have anything to
d him. Thor found a can of Pepsi someone had
around, but Tigran didn't seem to know how
drink from a straw.

"He'll be okay," I said. "Don't worry."

But he wasn't. We got onstage and the three
ngs came in with their presents. Just as the third
ng put down his gift, I made my monster face. I
as really close to Tigran, so it wasn't like he
uldn't see me. But instead of laughing the way
e always does, he just sat there, looking like he
as going to cry! I made the face again and he
st looked worse. Oh, boy! I was afraid they
ight not let me graduate sixth grade for wreck-
ng the senior play. Then all of a sudden Thor did
omething really smart for a change. It could
ave been a dumb thing to do, but it turned out to
e smart. He tilted up the sheep's head he had on
so Tigran could see his face, and he said "Baaaa"
as loud as he could. Tigran looked at him, surprised, and then roared with laughter, like it was
the funniest thing he ever saw. Then the audience
started to laugh too. You couldn't tell if it was

because of Thor's "Baaaa" or because of Tigran's laugh. Anyhow, Gerty was pleased.

When we came offstage, she hugged Tigran. "Terrific," she said. "That was marvelous."

Kim kissed Thor and me.

Thor looked really pleased with himself. "Just got to use the old noggin," he said. "Even if you are cast as a sheep."

"Okay, it *was* a good idea," I admitted, "but it *could* have been a mess."

"He likes animal sounds," Thor said. "Remember when I once pretended to be a dog?"

When we came back to our class, everyone rushed over and said how great we were. Our teacher said we'd showed how it wasn't how big your part was, it was what you did with it. The girls all crowded around Tigran while we waited for his mother to come and get him.

"He was a big hit?" she asked when she showed up.

"Sensational," Thor said. "He has a great laugh."

Eve had been standing next to me, playing with Tigran. She said she was going back to Venezuela and she didn't know if she'd be at our school next year. "I might come back for eighth grade," she said.

I'm just exactly Eve's height now. If she comes back in a year, I bet I'll be taller.

"I could write to you," she said.

"Okay," I said.

"I like to write letters," she said. "Do you?"

I thought. "Sure, pretty much." Writing to someone in a foreign country could be interesting. You could learn about foreign customs and stuff like that. I wonder if they have Leap Year in Venezuela. Anyway, I can always save the stamps.

While I was standing there, thinking about that, she leaned over really quickly and kissed me. I turned red. I don't think anyone was watching. "So have a good year, Robbie," she said.

"You too."

The rest of the day I thought about Eve's kissing me. I thought about how Thor had said I should've asked her to show me what she looked like without clothes on. Still, I'm not that sorry I didn't. If she comes back when she's thirteen, I can ask her then. Then she'll have more of a figure so there'll be more point to it. Maybe by then I'll actually be going out with girls. I'll have learned what to say to them.

The next morning I slept late, later than I would have if I'd had to go to school. When I came into the kitchen, Mom was there in her running shorts and shirt. There was a guy with her, also in shorts.

"Robbie, this is Arnold," Mom said.

Arnold was short and had fuzzy brownish hair. He reminded me of a koala bear, I'm not sure why. His ears stuck out a little. "Hi, Robbie," he said. He took a glass of juice Mom gave him.

"Arnold just started running too," Mom said. "The first day out, he saw me and thought I'd been doing it for months. He felt really good that he could pass me. Then he found out I'm a rank beginner."

"You're getting faster already, Ellen," Arnold said. "You just have to learn to pace yourself."

"I know," Mom said. "I charge forward and all of a sudden I get so winded, I have to stop."

"It's all in the pacing," Arnold said.

Maybe Arnold is going to be Mom's boyfriend. I hope so. At least then she won't be lonely while I'm at camp. With me around she isn't that lonely, but by herself she might be.

After Arnold left, Mom came into my room and said we should start shopping for things for my camp. "Nina's going to the same camp," I said. "The girls' part." Then all of a sudden I stopped. I realized that was a dumb thing to say.

"Who's Nina?" Mom asked.

"Some girl from my school," I said.

"Oh." Mom gazed at me. "Arnold's son has some of his camp stuff, Robbie," she said. "Would you mind using stuff that was already used? It would save a lot of money."

"I don't mind," I said.

"He has a sixteen-year-old son," she said. "Can you believe it? He *really* married young.

At least he doesn't have a daughter. It seems like practically everybody has a daughter my age. There must've been a lot of girls born that year. I don't know. I don't think I can handle any more girls.

18

Just before I left for camp, I got a letter from Tracie. It said:

Dear Robbie,

I'm going to be in a show this summer. Did you know that? It's called "The Princess and the Rascal." I'm a little girl who gets lost. I don't say anything, but I'm onstage a lot. I have to cry. I know how to cry. I learned how. It's a secret, but I'll tell you when I see you. I'll tell you one more secret. I like you better than your friend. I like you better than any boy I know. I think you're purfect. Do you think I am too? I hope you have a good summer.

Your girl friend,

Tracie ♡

143

P.S. Will you come to my show in the fall if it's still running? I can get you a ticket.

That's not how you spell perfect. I used to spell it that way when I was in third grade, but my teacher kept correcting it. One thing I know: I'm not perfect. There are a lot of things wrong with me. I guess Tracie doesn't know me that well. Or maybe if you like someone a lot, you think they're perfect. I guess, if that's true, it means I don't like anyone that much, because I don't think any girl I know right now is perfect. Some of them are pretty nice, but none of them are perfect. I guess I can ask Tracie to show me what she looks like if I want. But I better wait a few years.

Dad came in while I was reading Tracie's letter. He saw her name on the envelope: Perrin. "Isn't that—wasn't that Ellen's—"

I nodded. "He used to be," I said.

"Well, he didn't seem like Ellen's type," Dad said. "A bit offbeat, I thought."

I wondered what Mom's type was. Not Dad, I guess, or she wouldn't have gotten divorced from him. Not Paul, or they wouldn't have split up. Arnold? "She's going to be in a show," I said.

Dad looked surprised. "Ellen?"

"Tracie, Paul's daughter. She said she'd get me a ticket."

144

Dad smiled. "Pursued by women," he said. "And here I sit, forlorn, alone. . . ."

I made a face. I could tell he was joking. "How about Marilyn, Dad?" I said.

"Marilyn Sussman?" Dad snorted.

"Sure. What's wrong with her?"

He laughed. "Trying to sic Marilyn Sussman on me, huh?"

"I'm not trying to sic her on you. I thought you liked her."

Dad shrugged. He looked at me for a long time. "I have a friend in England," he said. "I'm going over to visit her this summer."

"England?"

He nodded. "She's someone I knew in college. Helen. She married an Englishman. We used to be in love with each other."

"So how come you didn't marry her?"

"She fell in love with someone else. These things happen, Robbie. Perfect synchrony is rare in these matters. Why, I don't know, why it should be so rare. But it is. . . . Helen met Nathaniel and I, eventually, met your mother."

"Maybe you shouldn't have gotten divorced," I said all of a sudden. "Maybe that was a dumb thing to do."

He was silent. "Well . . ."

"You could still move back with us," I said. "Then I wouldn't have to go back and forth all

145

the time and go to the wrong side because I get mixed up about where I'm supposed to be."

"*Do* you get mixed up?" Dad said. "I didn't know that."

"Not a lot," I said. "Sometimes."

"Robbie, it's—"

"Why don't you just ask Mom?" I suggested. "She gets lonely too sometimes, you know."

Dad looked sad. "Yes, I know."

"So, are you going to ask her, Dad?"

"I can't, Rob."

"Why not?"

"It wouldn't work."

"Why not?"

"For the same reasons it didn't the first time. We're the same people—we haven't changed."

"What's wrong with you?" I said.

"What do you mean?"

"How come you can't get along?"

"It's not that," Dad said. "Ellen may well be a terrific wife for someone someday, and who knows, maybe even I might be able to make someone happy. But together—"

I grinned at him. "Together you're a mess, huh?"

"Robbie?"

"What?"

"I'll miss you."

"I think I'll like camp," I said, getting up.

146

"Sure," Dad said. "You'll like it. Worry not."

Mom thought camp was the best part of her childhood. "It's so great, Robbie," she said. "The campfires, roasting marshmallows, telling ghost stories. You make friends you'll be friendly with thirty years from now."

I don't know that that's so important to me. Thirty years from now who knows where I'll be. If I get to be a doctor and cure something important, I might be rich and famous. I might be interviewed on TV. I might be living in a big house with a swimming pool. Or I might just be an explorer, off in some jungle. I might even be married with kids. I don't know who I'd want to marry, if I get married. Someone reasonably pretty and reasonably nice. Not somebody who likes to fight a lot. Maybe someone who can play chess.

Mom said she was going to drive to Vermont with Arnold. "His sister lives up there, right in the mountains," she said. "It's peaceful and quiet. . . . Don't worry about camp, Robbie. You'll have a great time."

"I'm not worried," I said.

"The first time is always scary," Mom said, "with anything."

"Mom?"

"Yeah?"

"Will you be okay when I'm not here?"

Mom smiled. "Why, sure, Robbie."

"I just thought you might get lonely or something."

"I'll be fine."

I wanted to say something to Mom about how I was sorry I'd introduced Paul to Jill, but I didn't know what to say. "Dad's going to England," I said.

"Good," Mom said. "He looks like he needs a vacation. He's been looking tired."

Monday morning was the day Mom was supposed to take me down to Port Authority Bus Terminal. That's where my bus leaves from for camp. I had everything packed. I spoke to Thor the night before. He's not going to camp. He'll just be at his parents' country place. I told him how Paul's daughter was going to be at the camp I was going to.

"The one with the braid? Boy, you're lucky."

"No, the other one."

"Oh."

"She's nice. I like her."

"Which one?"

"Not as a girl friend," I said. "She's just nice to talk to."

"The one with the braid?"

"No! The other one."

"What's the name of the one with the braid?"

"Tracie."

148

"I never saw a girl who was that pretty," he said. "The thing is, she might be at her peak. That's what Derek says."

"At ten?"

"Derek says some of them go downhill pretty fast. . . ."

"Hey, Thor, have a good summer, okay?"

"Sure, you too. . . . Don't get lost in the woods."

I laughed. I hoped I wouldn't.

It was kind of a mob scene at Port Authority. It's good they had a sign for my camp, because there were a lot of other camps with a lot of other kids roaming around. Mom was carrying one of my bags and I was carrying the duffel bag with all the blankets and stuff in it. She hugged me. I was afraid she might do that. She gets kind of tearful at times like this. Luckily a lot of the other mothers were doing the same thing, and anyway no one knew me.

"Have a wonderful time," Mom said, sniffing.

"I guess I better get on the bus," I said.

Just as I was walking toward the bus, I felt someone yank on my sleeve. I turned around. It was Dad. I'd told him when I was leaving, but he'd said he wasn't sure he could get away from work to come down. He threw his arms around me in a big hug.

149

"Remember it's only for the summer," he whispered.

I nodded. "Have a good time in England, Dad."

"I'll try, Robbie."

I got on the bus. I was lucky. I got a seat near the window. If I sit near the window, I don't get carsick so much. Mostly I get carsick in cars, but I can get carsick on buses too. A boy came over and stood next to me. "Is anybody sitting here?" he asked.

I shook my head.

He sat down next to me. "Hey, can I have the window?" he said.

I hesitated. "I get carsick," I said.

"Me too."

"You can have it half the time, okay?"

"Thanks." He looked at me. "It's my first year at this camp."

"Yeah, me too."

He leaned forward and looked out the window. "Those're my parents," he said. "The ones right in front. That's my dog with them."

I looked out. I saw this couple standing off to one side, holding a collie on a leash. I looked around. "Those are mine," I said, pointing. "That man in the blue shirt and that woman with the curly hair."

"Yeah, I see them."

I guess he couldn't tell they were divorced or anything. They looked just like two regular parents.

The bus started up. I waved out the window. Mom and Dad stood there, waving back at me until the bus pulled out of sight.

ABOUT THE AUTHOR

Norma Klein was born in New York City and graduated cum laude and a member of Phi Beta Kappa from Barnard College with a degree in Russian. She later received a master's degree in Slavic languages from Columbia University.

Ms. Klein began publishing short stories while attending Barnard College and since then has written over 25 books for readers of all ages. The author gets her ideas for her books from everyday life and advises would-be writers to do the same—to write simply and honestly about their experiences or things they really care about.

Several of Norma Klein's books are available from Archway Paperbacks, including *A Honey of a Chimp, Hiding, Naomi in the Middle, What It's All About,* and *Tomboy.* She received the Child Study Children's Book Committee at Bank Street College Award for *What It's All About.*

Ms. Klein lives in New York City with her husband and their two daughters.